In a Pig's Eye

Published by Airplane Books

A Kip Yardley mystery
© 2018 Don Yarber

ISBN-13: 978-0-9850695-5-1

In a Pig's Eye

Don Yarber

Copyright © June 5, 2018 Don Yarber
ISBN-13: 978-0-9850695-5-1

Prologue

The starving pigs charged with slobbers hanging from open mouths. The first one to reach the man lowered its massive head and jabbed two tusks into the soft tissue of the belly. The boar raised its head, ripping the intestines and part of the rib cage. Blood sprayed into the air, arousing primal instincts in the rest of the beasts. In seconds they consumed nearly all of the midsection, and squealing incessantly, they fought each other for the heart, lungs and remaining parts.

CHAPTER 1

I could hear the music blaring from somewhere as I parked my Cadillac in front of the house, at the end of the cul-de-sac, tree lined street. The number painted on the curb agreed with the number on the piece of paper I had scotch taped to the dash board.

The Caddy was an old one, a 1952 Convertible, powder blue, with white leather seats and a white top. I had the top down as it was scorching hot in Simi-Valley, California on August 10th.

The house was relatively new in a tract of new homes that had been built on the site of a former lettuce farm. Simi-Valley city had its beginning in the early 1960s when developers decided that no matter where you worked around Los Angeles, there were enough freeways to get you to your job from Simi-Valley. Shortly afterward, homes started springing up and selling in the low $20's. The same homes were now selling for $850,000 and up.

I had my office in Santa Monica and wouldn't want to live in Simi, but a $1500 fee for one night as a security agent for a party was enough to make me drive the 50 miles or so.

I got out of the Caddy and walked up the sidewalk to slump stone walls with a wrought iron gate guarding the entrance to the home. A lighted doorbell was encased in the frame of the heavy wrought iron gate, and I punched it twice.

The dame that came to the door in a thong bikini could have stepped out of a Veronica's Secrets catalogue. She was about five feet and five or six inches tall, very curvaceous. Long black hair hung down in damp ringlets around her well tanned shoulders.

"Hi," I said. "I'm Kip Yardley. I'll be your security agent tonight."

"Come in," she said, smiling. "I'm Monique. I'm Mr. Sanders personal assistant."

I wondered what duties a personal assistant performed, but let it slide. Business only, I reminded myself.

She unlocked the gate and let it swing in. I stepped through and closed it behind me. It clanged as it locked.

"Come in, please. I'll introduce you to Mr. Sanders."

I followed her up two steps and onto a Mexican tiled small front porch. She opened the front door and held it open for me, her long, tanned arm extended to her side. As I entered, she stepped slightly towards me and I felt my bare arm brush across the fabric of the top of her bikini. Firm breasts, barely concealed by the fabric, jiggled slightly as I brushed against them and stepped into the entry way of Rod Sander's home.

He sat in a wheel chair with his back to me.

"Mr. Sanders. this is Mr. Yardley, the security agent for the party."

I heard the quiet hum of a small electric motor and the wheel chair spun in a half circle so that he faced me. He smiled a broad pearly smile that accentuated his dark handlebar mustache.

"Come in," he said. "I'm glad you are here a little early. I can brief you on what I expect of you."

"Let's hear it," I said.

"Sit down," he motioned to a plush sectional chair covered with a maroon colored fabric that felt like fur of some kind. I couldn't think of any animal that had that natural maroon color, so I just sat.

"There will be fifty guests, providing they all show. Approximately 30 men, 20 women. Drinks will be served at a bar by an experienced bartender, and hors-d'oeuvres will be served by a caterer with a staff of three including the owner."

"All I really want you to do is to make sure that none of the guests get overly argumentative. If there is any sign of a fight, get the trouble makers outside. There's a gate at the back by the pool, take them there and make sure that they don't get back in."

"No problem," I said.

"You don't look like most security agents I've hired in the past," he said.

"What are you looking for?"

"Size. Most have been big Dudes, 6 four or five, 230 pounds or more, all muscle."

"Looks are deceiving," I said, as he stared at my 5 foot 11 inch frame and gave a quick look over my 175 pounds of flesh.

"What exactly are your qualifications?" He asked.

"You should know, you hired me."

"Actually Monique hired you," he said. "At my direction, of course. I think she got your number from the yellow pages. What makes you capable of breaking up a fight, let's say between two big guys?"

"Monique didn't ask." I said. "And my number isn't in the yellow pages."

"I'm asking." He said, his smile fading fast.

"I don't discuss my qualifications after I'm hired, only before," I told him. "Now if you don't want my services here tonight, I'll take my $250 cancellation fee, and you can go back to the yellow pages. I think I can still make the Dodger's ballgame."

"No, no. There's no need for that," he said hastily. "I was just wondering. You agreed to work unarmed. I do not want any gunplay, not even any weapons shown. Agreed?"

"Fine," I said, "I'm not carrying a weapon."

"Well, now that we understand each other, you can have a seat out by the pool, help yourself to food and drink. The guests should start arriving in a half hour."

CHAPTER 2

I sat in a chaise lounge near the pool, in the shade of the 6 ft slump stone wall that encompassed the back yard. The pool was big for Simi-Valley standards. With the drought and water rationing, most pool owners were starting to cringe at the added surcharge to keep water in the pools. I estimated the pool to be forty by twenty. It took up the biggest part of the yard, only a small cabaña dressing room against the back wall, and a six foot swath of St. Augustine grass down one side, separated by three huge fan palms. The slump stone wall went all around the yard. Along the wall hung pool cleaning equipment, attached to hooks embedded in the slump stone. A sign stood out in the center of the equipment: "WE DON'T SWIM IN YOUR TOILET, PLEASE DON'T PEE IN OUR POOL".

I didn't like the music that was blaring through speakers on the corner of the cabaña, but I wasn't getting paid to like it. It was seventies disco music. I would have preferred jazz or classical guitar. But it wasn't my party.

Guests started arriving, a few scattered couples here and there at first and then a crowd of people. Bikini clad women and big hairy dudes soon occupied most of the free space around the pool. I sipped on a Dos Equis and had a couple of sandwiches of some kind of cheese and white bread with the crusts cut off.

The party was in full swing when Rod Sanders showed up on the patio with a white Hawaiian style shirt and a pair of blue bathing trunks. He rolled around greeting people, one hand on the controls of his wheel chair and the other holding a drink that looked like a Mai Tai.

Things were quiet enough and I was beginning to think that I would spend the entire evening ogling beautiful women in their bikinis, and not have to earn my fee. Wrong.

My eyes caught a man and a woman in a seemingly strong disagreement, close to the rear of the lot, not far from the gate Sanders had mentioned. The man had his hand raised, palm out facing the woman as if to say, "Stop it" but if that was what he meant, it wasn't working. Her mouth was going forty miles an hour and although I'm no lip reader, I think I saw the "F" word lip-synced a few hundred times. I got up and meandered towards them. A short haired blond beauty asked me if I wanted to dance and I said, "No Thanks" and she said, "What're you gay?" and I let it slide and kept walking slowly towards the couple who were now definitely in a hot debate.

Rod Sanders was in front of me, his wheelchair humming its almost inaudible tune. I stepped aside and passed him and walked quickly to the couple who were arguing. I could hear them now, every other word a cuss word, voices rising on each inflection. I stopped behind the man and listened for just a few seconds.

".....I'll go with whoever I want to go with, you stupid shit," the female was saying.

"I'll knock your damned teeth down your throat if you even mention his name again," the man said.

"Cory, Cory, Cory..." she said, mocking him.

He drew back a huge fist and started to launch it at her mocking mouth. I caught his wrist, jerked downward and quickly stepped to my left, bringing his arm up behind his back.

"Hold on, pal," I said.

I didn't expect the results of my action. He was a lot bigger than my five eleven one seventy five. He spun to his left dragging me around like I was a rat terrier hanging to the neck of a Saint Bernard. My right leg hit something hard and I heard a sound like rubber squealing on concrete. That wasn't unusual since it was rubber squealing on concrete.

It was Rod Sander's wheel chair, moving over the edge of the pool, tipping as if in slow motion.

Rod's drink was flying through the air and I almost forgot what I should do with the big guy who was whirling me around.

Almost, but not quite. Years of Martial Arts training took over automatically. I slid my hand to his and quickly found his index and pinky fingers and bent them back towards his wrist, not far enough to break them, but far enough to take the fight out of him. I kept the pressure until he was on his knees.

The woman screamed and then several women screamed.

They guy grunted and swore at me. I glanced to my right.

Rod Sanders was on his way to the bottom of his swimming pool, his motor driven wheel chair on top of him.

I released my grip on the ape's fingers and dove into the pool. The wheel chair was sinking faster than Sanders and clunked him on the head as he neared the bottom. I reached him in seconds and grabbed him by the collar of his white Hawaiian shirt. Two strong kicks and we were at the surface. As my head broke water I saw the couple who had been arguing moving towards the gate in the back wall, the man had both of her hands pinned behind her back.

I'm not a strong swimmer but it was relatively easy to reach the pool edge where waiting hands pulled Rod Sanders from the water. He had a small cut on his head where the wheel chair had hit him and it was bleeding. Red stains appeared on his white shirt.

As I climbed out of the pool I heard the motor of a car start and the screech of rubber on concrete from behind the wall. I stepped to the gate and opened it. The car was a Pontiac Firebird, license number AAH 374.

I filed that information away in file 13. My first concern was for my client and I turned him over on his back and made sure he was breathing. "I'm very sorry, Mr. Sanders," I said.

"What happened?" he asked.

I told him exactly what had occurred. The argument, my catching the man's arm to keep him from creaming the woman. The spin, the wheel chair going out and over the edge of the pool.

"Will someone please get my chair," he said.

I walked around the edge of the pool and took a long pole with a hook on the end from the hanger. I managed to get the hook through the spokes of the right wheel and maneuvered it to shallow water, then to the steps. When I brought it back to Sanders he was sitting up, his useless legs dangling over the edge of the pool. I got him under his shoulders and lifted him into a sitting position in the wheel chair. I noticed that his legs did not seem atrophied from lack of use, but let it slide.

"Thank you," he said. "I guess I owe you more than your regular fee, you saved my life. Your clothes are soaked and your cell phone is probably ruined."

"I hope the rest of your party goes smoother," I said. "I'm sorry that I bumped your wheel chair into the pool."

"We'll talk about it later," he told me. It made me wonder if he had intentions of paying me more or paying me less for allowing the goon to swing me around and knock the wheel chair out of control.

The tall blond with the short hair was standing near me.

"Now will you dance with me?" she asked.

"I don't dance," I said. "Thanks, anyway."

"Screw you, jerk!" She muttered and walked away.

I returned to the chaise lounge where I had sat before the arguing couple had caused me to meander into the crowd. Things had settled almost to normal. Some guests were dancing to the seventies music, others stood with drinks in hands, trying to make conversation over the blaring of the speakers. I watched the crowd slowly settle back into the routine of partying, sipped on another Dos Equis and relaxed, as much as it is possible to relax while in wet clothes.

By 11 p.m. guests had drifted out of the pool area and into the house and by 12 they had said their goodnights and left the party. Only a few stragglers were still wishing their host a good night, telling him that they enjoyed the party, and glancing at their cell phones. Rod Sanders was cordially playing the perfect host, thanking his guests for coming, wishing them goodnights and "drive safely".

When the last guest had gone, his personal assistant, Monique, asked me to come in. My clothes had long since dried. Sanders sat in a chair sipping on a drink.

"I want to thank you again for coming, Mr. Yardley," he said. "And for saving my life."

"I'm glad your party was a success, Mr. Sanders," I said. "And again, I apologize for the way I handled the situation that caused your accident."

"Think nothing of it," he smiled. "It was probably as much my fault. I saw the argument and thought I could calm them down. I should have left it to you, that's what I hired you for."

"Monique, please make out a check to Mr. Yardley." he said to his personal assistant. She walked to a desk and opened a drawer and got a check folder.

"Fifteen hundred, that's what we agreed on, wasn't it?" she asked me.

"Yes." I said and stood waiting.

"One more thing," Sanders said.

I waited.

"You impress me, Yardley, and I've checked with some of my contacts about your PI record, Are you interested in making $50 thousand?"

I was all ears. I hesitated, but not for long. "Depends," I said. "What do I have to do to earn it? I don't kill people, rob banks, or perform unholy acts with either men or women."

"Nothing like that," he said. "All I need is someone to go to Illinois and bring back a suitcase."

"I don't deal in drugs, either," I said.

"No drugs."

"What's in it? A body?"

He laughed.

"Nothing like that either," he said. "I won't tell you what is in it, just that it is valuable. When you bring it to me I will verify that it is indeed the suitcase I want, then I'll give you a check for $50 thousand."

My mind raced wildly. A bomb? Plans for an invention that would change coal into diamonds? Jewelry worth millions? I was thinking that if it were worth $50 thousand for my courier fee, it must be worth several times that much.

"Interested?" he asked.

"Yes." I said. "I'll let you know on Monday." Today was Saturday, and I wanted to think about it for a while. I wanted to run down some information on Rod Sanders to see if I could determine what might be in a suitcase that he was willing to pay me fifty grand to fetch.

"OK," he said. "I'll expect a call from you by ten on Monday, then. If I don't hear from you by that time, I'll find someone else."

"Fair enough," I said. "Good night, Mr. Sanders."

CHAPTER 3

I was intrigued so much by the offer I had received from Rod Sanders that I couldn't sleep after I got back to my apartment in Santa Monica. I took my cell phone apart and put it in a jar of rice.

I got on the computer and did a background search on Sanders. I pay a healthy sum each month for a service that checks very thoroughly on people. It gives me pretty much everything I want to know, including relatives, their police records, addresses where the subject has lived, employment history, licenses held, and whether or not they are sex offenders.

Sanders was clean. He had no record with the Police Departments in any city he had lived. He was a 15 year resident of Simi-Valley, self employed as a computer repair technician. He owned a small shop in the heart of the city and drove to and from work in a specially equipped van. There was a former Mrs. Rod Sanders, a Hollywood extra who had divorced him. I made a note of her address and telephone number.

I checked if he had ever lived in Illinois and learned that he had been born in Peoria, the pig capitol of the world. More pork is processed in Peoria than any other city in the U.S. and probably the entire world. I remember driving through the area south of Peoria once, years past, and could still almost smell the stench. No matter how you say it, pig crap stinks. It occurred to me that the Muslim communities might be asking courts to ban the pig farms completely. Peoria citizens had already got court orders limiting the distance of a pig farm from private residences. The FDA had issued rules on sanitation, as if anything can make a pig farm sanitary.

Sanders had played football in high school, then Notre Dame as quarterback, and suffered a back injury. The report gave no severity of the injury, but I assumed it was the reason Sanders was confined to a wheel chair.

Maybe the suitcase had something to do with his family, ancestors or land records. Maybe he owned half of Peoria and could prove it if he found the records. Maybe the sun would come up tomorrow if I got off of the damned computer and went to bed.

I checked a schedule that had been given to me by a friend of mine, Toby Smith, of the CHP, to see if he was on duty. It showed that he was off until

Monday. I wanted to talk to him about the offer before I called Sanders, to see if he could shed any light on either Sanders or the offer. Oh well, I guess I would just have to make a decision without Toby's advice.

Toby and I have been friends since college days. He was instrumental in helping me solve my first big case when an ex-CHP officer, and owner of several strip bars, was gunned down.

I turned off the computer and went to bed.

Sunday morning I woke up with Sanders on my mind. The thing that occurred to me was that maybe his personal assistant, the lovely Monique, could tell me more about him. She was certainly a person that I would tell my life story to, if I had that opportunity. She was a very nice looking woman.

I showered and shaved and had a first cup of coffee. My cell phone had dried out from the dunking and appeared to be working fine. I found the number she had used to call me to book the security job. It was nearly nine o'clock on Sunday morning.

The phone rang twice before she picked up.

"Hello."

"Good morning, Monique, this is Kip Yardley."

"Is there something wrong, Mr. Yardley? Her voice sounded as if she were wide awake.

"No, nothing like that," I said. "I have been pondering Mr. Sanders offer and just needed to ask a few questions."

"I'm at my home," she said. "Mr. Sanders is at his home. I can give you his number if you'd like it."

"Actually I wanted to talk to you," I said. "Maybe you'd like to join me for brunch?"

"This is about Mr. Sanders offer, and you want to talk to me? Shouldn't you be talking directly to him?"

"OK," I confessed. "You've got me. I really wanted to see you again, and thought I might consult with you regarding Mr. Sanders. I can meet you somewhere for brunch or perhaps come by and pick you up."

"I haven't had brunch at El Torritos in quite some time," she said. "If you can pick me up in an hour, I'll agree to brunch. I'm not sure about talking to you regarding my employer, however."

Something is better than nothing, I thought.

"Tell me where to pick you up, I'll be there," I said. Girl after my own heart. El Torritos is a Mexican Restaurant that I have grown to love. Their food is excellent and they serve complimentary champagne all day on Sunday's. A fiver in the hands of the right waiter or bus-boy will get the bottle left on your table, and replaced with a full one when it runs dry.

She gave me her address. It wasn't in Simi-Valley, but Thousand Oaks, a community bordering the valley. Depending on traffic, I thought I could be there in an hour.

"I'll be there by ten," I said.

"OK," she replied. "See you."

I hung up and started looking for something to wear. Being a bachelor has its drawbacks. When all of your underwear is dirty, you wash. When all of your sheets are dirty, you wash. When all of your dishes and silverware are dirty, you wash. I wasn't quite that bad, but no-one was picking up and tidying up after me. I could have had someone come in and clean the place once a week but you never know who you can trust. Not that I had anything to hide, but client confidentiality is something I take seriously and although all of my files are at my office, I occasionally bring something home to go over at my leisure. That is the reason I do my own cleanup and only once in a while send my laundry out. I never know when I will leave notes in shirt pockets. I carry a small notebook and jot things down that I think are important, and I've been known to leave it in my shirt or jeans pocket.

I picked up the shirt and pants I had worn the night before, removed my wallet that was still wet from the pool episode, my keys, and my notebook, also wet, and put them on the night stand. I found a clean pair of Dockers and a golf shirt and clean underwear. I stuffed keys, wallet and notebook in the clean Dockers. I was out the door in five minutes.

CHAPTER 4

We sipped champagne as we waited for a table, and I limited my small talk to questions about Monique. She was talkative enough as long as I kept the conversation going about her. Her past, her likes and dislikes, her.

She didn't ask about me, and I wasn't surprised at that, she probably had checked me out thoroughly before hiring me for Sanders' party. Once in a while she would tiptoe around the subject of whether or not I was married, going with someone, or casually involved. Nothing direct, but enough to tell me that she was interested.

I didn't volunteer any information. Most of what I wanted to talk about was Rod Sanders.

"Have you worked for Sanders long?"

"I really don't work for Sanders," she said. "I'm employed by a company that provides home nursing services. Mr. Sanders is my current assignment. I do things for him that are more in the line of a secretary, but also look after his personal comfort, make sure he is getting his meals and help him exercise."

"And how long have you been doing that?" I asked.

"Since college," she said. "I got my nursing degree two years ago."

"So you've known Mr. Sanders for two years?" She was being a little evasive in her answers.

"Oh no," she said, smiling. "I've only known him for a month. I thought you were talking about how long I've worked for home nursing services."

"Does he have company other than parties?"

"Once a man came and they talked for about an hour," she said. "I was a little concerned because they seemed to be arguing about something.. Their voices raised to a point that I could hear them through the closed door of Mr. Sanders office."

"Was that at his place of business or at his home?"

"It was at the shop," she said. "I go there at ten each day, Monday through Friday, and stay until two. I just keep track of his health issues, and keep a log. He asked me to pose as his personal secretary for the party to impress his guests."

"Do you know what caused his paralysis?" I asked.

"I believe it was a football injury," she replied.

Our table was ready and we moved to the dining area. A busboy named Nacho who was in his fifties, married and had ten kids in Mexico, brought a fresh bottle of champagne to our table. He was very talkative and I tipped him with a five and the bottle stayed on the table.

"So the man that spent an hour in Sanders' office was disturbed about something?"

"They didn't start off arguing, of course I didn't know what they were discussing, but towards the end of his stay, the man's voice became very loud. There were a few "f" words yelled. The man seemed highly upset about something."

"Do you think it might have concerned the former Mrs. Rod Sanders?"

"No, I don't think so." She said. "The way I understand it, Mr. Sanders' ex-wife severed all ties years ago, and they never see each other."

"What did the guy look like? How was he dressed?"

"He was a big guy. Looked like a boxer or bouncer or something. His nose looked like it had been broken once, it was slightly off center, kind of like that news announcer, what's his name? Williams or something like that."

"Might he have been a cop?"

"I don't think so," she said. "He was dressed nice. A blue suit and white shirt. No tie. Tattoo up the side of his neck, and on to the side of his face. The left side, if I remember correctly."

"How about at his home, did he have visitors there? Women?"

"A woman came one day when I was just leaving," she said. "Very attractive lady,

appeared to be a little too old for Mr. Sanders, though. More like in her fifties."

We had nearly finished eating when she quit talking. I learned a lot about Sanders but still had no idea what a suitcase might contain that he was willing to pay fifty grand to have me fetch it for him.

I took her home and turned down an offer to have a beer "or something" in her apartment. The champagne had been enough for me to drink in one morning, and I didn't like the idea of mixing it with beer or "something else". There is a time and a place for everything. This wasn't it.

CHAPTER 5

I took the offer. Monday I called Rod Sanders and said that I'd take the job. I had some caveats, however. If I went to Illinois and was unable to find the suitcase or unable to bring it back, I would collect 10 percent of the $50 thousand. He agreed. Illinois is a big place and I had to have some idea where to find the illusive suitcase. He gave me the address of a house that he said he owned out in the country, near pig city. It was a small two bedroom place surrounded by cornfields and occupied by a young couple in their thirties to whom Sanders had leased the place. They knew nothing of the suitcase or its whereabouts, he assured me. It was hidden behind a false partition in the attic of the old house. He gave me a letter of introduction and in the letter designated me as his "property management" representative. I was there to perform an inspection of the property per the lease agreement.

According to the letter, I had his permission to remove any item from the premises that did not belong to the lessee, including, but not limited to, furniture, luggage, bedding, clothing or unplanted (potted) plants.

He had a contract ready for me to sign. It stipulated that I was hired to perform a courier service, to wit: to pick up a man's large, brown, leather Samsonite suitcase at an address provided by him. He had inserted a picture of a suitcase on page two of the contract. To return the suitcase to his Simi-Valley business address unopened. He would know if it had been opened as it was padlocked and sealed with a wire and plastic seal. I was sworn to secrecy (by terms of the contract) and could not tell anyone of my mission. My firm would only know the city of my destination, my departure date, and my expected date of return. I was also forbidden to discuss my fee with anyone other than my tax accountant, doing so would result in a breach of contract and revocation of the fee in its entirety

I signed the contract in his office and watched as he motored his wheel chair to a small safe in the rear of his shop, spun the dial a few times, and locked the contract inside. Whatever was in that suitcase meant a lot to him to go to such precautions. It had bothered me all along, but my curiosity got the better of me. So did the $50 thousand. I folded my copy of the contract till it fit in my jeans pocket and stuffed it there.

Back at my office I called Continental and made arrangements to fly to Peoria. I'd thought once about driving and stopping in Flagstaff to visit an old friend. I'd nearly gotten myself killed working on a murder case for him a few years past, and thought about playing a round of golf or two. Then I realized that my contract had a time clause in it and since "time is of the essence" in most contracts, decided to fly to Peoria, rent a car, and fly back when done.

Early Tuesday morning I was at 30,000 feet on my way to Peoria. I flew coach but bribed a ticket agent to get me the seat right behind the first class partition so I had plenty of leg room. As soon as the Captain turned off the "fasten seat belts" sign, I ordered a Bloody Mary from the flight attendant and opened my laptop, did a MapQuest search for the address of the farm house I needed to visit, and brought it up on the screen.

I memorized the directions from the Peoria airport, then switched the browser to Google Earth and did a search for the same address. I was able to zoom in to a picture of the front of the house. It was an old farm home, frame construction. The front appeared to be covered with asbestos shingles, common in the early 1930's. A porch ran the full width of the house front, three steps from ground level to the porch floor. There were no curtains on the windows and the yard was in a state of disarray. An old model Chevrolet Monte Carlo sat in the yard with blocks under the frame and no wheels on the rear. A child's bicycle with a flat tire leaned against the Chevy. Papers and debris were strewn across the yard, grass hadn't been mowed in a month when the satellite passed high overhead and snapped this picture from 80 miles up.

It seemed funny to me that the United States had the technology to photograph any house in the country with such detail that you could read the license number on an old Chevy Monte Carlo, yet we couldn't find cells of terrorist in Iraq, Afghanistan, or Pakistan. Sometimes I wondered if we really wanted to find the damned terrorist. Without them there wouldn't be a need for war and the Washington hawks and their cronies who manufacture planes and bombs wouldn't be as wealthy.

I read through a golf magazine and the travel magazine before getting to Denver. The plane landed and people got off and more got on, then we taxied out and took off again. Next stop, Peoria. I was getting tired of reading and had already seen the in-flight movie, so I reclined my seat as far as it would go and in minutes was sawing logs, dreaming of hogs.

The subtle screech of tires hitting the runway woke me from my dream and I stretched my legs and sat patiently until the plane came to a stop. I gathered my carryon luggage from the overhead compartment and left the aircraft. Peoria. Pig capital of the world.

I stopped at the gate agent's desk and waited until they brought me a sealed envelope with my 9MM Ruger in it. Although I had a permit, regulations required that I surrender it to the crew and would receive it upon reaching my final destination. I had surrendered it in Los Angeles and was a bit anxious that it made the transfer in Denver. Lately I have taken a habit of carrying the gun, after being shot at several times, and facing hoods that meant business. I walked in the men's room, into a stall and after relieving myself, ripped open the envelope and put the gun in my shoulder holster. One of my more recent projects had been to get a concealed carry license in all but two states, Hawaii and Alaska.

At the luggage claim area I waited for my suitcase and a canvas bag with some tools I thought I might need to search for the suitcase in a false partition area.

Avis had my rental car waiting. It was an economy small Hyundai. It had a built in GPS and I took the time to key in the address of the farmhouse. I got a little confused leaving the airport but managed to get turned around and headed south on highway 474, the loop around Peoria, to Interstate 74, then 175 towards Tremont. I found the exit I was looking for about 45 minutes later and was soon driving a county highway through tall corn fields.

The GPS system was working fine and I followed its directions without effort. It had me turn off of the county highway on a local road. Now the corn was growing up to within a few feet of the road and all I could see was corn on both sides, and the road stretching west in front of me. Minutes later I turned south again on a gravel road and drove for a quarter of a mile until it dead ended in the front yard of the house I was seeking. The yard looked the same as the picture on Google Search except the car was gone. The bicycle lay on its side near where the car had been. Concrete blocks were exactly where the picture showed them, grass growing up around them. Papers and litter, beer cans and fast food bags were strewn here and there.

I pulled the rental to the right of the concrete blocks and parked it behind a garage sized shed that was in sad state of repairs. It was near five and I could hear whippoorwills singing somewhere in the distance. Other than their whip poor will notes, silence. I got the canvas bag from the trunk and walked to the porch, climbed the three concrete steps and heard my own hollow footsteps as I crossed the porch. I knocked several times and got no answer. The place looked deserted. No curtains on the dirty, streaked windows. I stepped to one nearest the door, shaded my eyes with my hand and peered inside. A rickety old divan sat forlornly in a corner on filthy shag carpet. Newspapers were scattered on the floor. I couldn't see any other sign of life or recent activity. A night stand next to the divan held an ashtray full of cigarette butts and an overturned beer can sidled up against it to keep from rolling off.

I tried the door. It wasn't locked so I pushed and it opened. No breaking and entering if the door isn't locked. Just entering. Inside, the place smelled of stale beer and cigarettes. I walked across the shag carpet, scuffing dust into the air with each step. A wide doorway opened into a kitchen area. A chrome dining room table was on my left and next to it a refrigerator sat humming in the silence. I tried the light switch and an overhead light came on. I switched it back off. It was still light enough that I could see perfectly well without it. If someone drove up in the yard the only indication of my presence would be the empty rental car behind the shed.

I sat the bag down on the table and looked around for an opening to the attic that was supposed to be in the kitchen. Sure enough there was a framed section of ceiling drywall directly over the table. Convenient, I thought.

A chromed chair with red naugahyde covering was also convenient. I thought briefly that a table and four of these chairs would sell for nearly a grand in an antique store. I pulled it over and climbed up on the table, raised my arms over my head and pushed up on the framed drywall section. It moved about three inches and I slid it to one side, reached down to the table and picked up the canvas bag with my tools, and set it inside the ceiling opening before pulling myself up into the attic.

I noticed the heat immediately. The late evening sun was beating on the window in the front part of the attic and the heat was stifling. I carefully crossed to the window, stepping where I knew there would be ceiling joists. On both sides of me, where the roof sloped to the low spot, were drywall partitions. If my instructions from Sanders were correct, there should be another partition behind the one on my right, and behind that I should find a suitcase.

I opened the window a foot and reversed my direction to the other end of the attic and opened a window there the same distance, immediately feeling the draft of cooler air. I took a portable saw from the canvas bag and had my finger on the trigger to turn it on when I heard a gunshot. It was a loud pop. I eased my way back to the front of the house, standing to the right of the window, and looked out. I saw a blue pickup truck that I hadn't heard pull into the yard. A man was running towards a barn fifty yards to the north of the house. Another man was running after him, shooting. Three more shots, the pop, pop, pop of an automatic pistol echoed in the attic.

The running man stopped running and turned with his hands in the air, arms outstretched.

I dug in my pants pocket and pulled out my cell phone. I pushed and held the "camera" button and watched.

"Don't shoot me," I heard him yell.

The shooter held the gun at arm's length and yelled.

"Get on the ground, keep your hands on your head!"

I gave a quick glance down at the opening to the attic and wondered if I should put the drywall piece back in place, if they came in the house they wouldn't know I was there. But my footprints on the chair and table would tell anyone but a blind man that I was in the attic.

Back to the scene below me. The man who had been running was now prone on the ground, his hands on his head. Shooter was standing over him, pointing the gun at the man's head. The sun was shining over the top of the barn roof, right in my eyes. All I could see was silhouettes, no faces.

"Last chance, Billy," I heard him say. "Where's the suitcase?"

"I'm telling you, I don't know."

"I'm going to count to five, Billy."

"I don't know where it is, I don't have it."

"One."

Billy squirmed and got to his hands and knees. "Please, I don't know. Please, Cory, I'd tell you if I knew, You've got to believe me."

"Two."

"I don't know...."

Suddenly Billy threw himself forward and wrapped his arms around Cory's legs, knocking him to the ground. I watched, fascinated, as Billy clambered for the gun.

Pow! I heard one last shot.

Both men lay on the ground for a full fifteen seconds.

I saw movement. Slowly one of them got up. The other one laid there, still as a corpse.

The man now standing was the one called Billy. He had miraculously saved his own life. He wore a short sleeved plaid shirt and blue jeans. He stuck the automatic in his back pocket. His stout torso bent forward and he flexed his knees and picked up the other man, Cory. He held Cory in a fireman's carry and moved towards a fence that ran perpendicular to the barn. I heard a low moan. Cory was still alive.

Billy tossed Cory over the fence like a sack of potatoes. Immediately I saw pigs scamper to the spot. The sight that I viewed and recorded on my cell phone was ghastly and one that will cause nightmares for the rest of my life. Below me a man was being eaten alive by pigs. I heard a horrendous scream.

The starving pigs charged with slobbers hanging from open mouths. The first one to reach the man lowered its massive head and jabbed two tusks into the soft tissue of the belly. The boar reared its head, ripping the intestines and part of the rib cage. Blood sprayed into the air, arousing primal instincts in the rest of the beasts. In seconds they consumed nearly all of the midsection, and squealing incessantly, they fought each other for the heart, lungs and remaining parts.

Blood sprayed like a fountain over him. My hands were shaking so much I almost dropped the cell phone. My gun was in my shoulder holster but before my shocked senses could force me to make an effort to get down out of the attic, Billy started the blue pickup truck with a roar and did a wheelie in the front yard. The back tires threw grass, gravel and dirt all the way up on the porch as the truck screamed away. I released the "record" button on my phone and stuck it in my pocket.

I got down as quickly as I could from the attic and ran to the fence where I had seen Billy toss Cory in to the pigs. There was a lot of blood at a spot not 4 feet from the fence. I could see bits of flesh and torn clothing, the pigs had scattered the body over a half acre. I thought I could see a head being pushed around by three large pigs. I took some pictures of the mess with my phone, returned to the house and looked for something to drink in the refrigerator. I found some bottled water in the fridge and a bottle of Jack Daniels in the cupboard, about a fourth remaining. I found a glass in a second cupboard and poured the whiskey, added water and drank it down.

My hands were still shaking, and my mind was racing. I'd just watched a man eaten alive by hogs, nothing I had ever seen in my life was so frightening and gruesome. Now I had to make a choice. Either I call the police and tell them what I saw, or get the suitcase and get the hell out of there.

All of my training in law enforcement told me I should call the police. All of my life experiences told me to get the suitcase and get out. As a witness to a murder, and the last person to see the victim alive, I would be detained. My reason for being on the premises would have to be discussed, police would question me about that, and I had a contract that forbade me from talking about it. If I told anyone the real reason for my trip to Peoria, I would be out everything, flight expenses, car rental, the whole deal.

If I got the suitcase and managed to survive long enough to get it back to Rod Sanders, I'd get my 50 grand. Then I could pursue the murder of Cory. I could inform the authorities in Los Angeles and let them communicate the details. Chances are I would not be detained in LA.

By the time I made up my mind it was getting dark. I had no desire to go rummaging around a vacant house after dark, if I turned on lights they would be visible to anyone approaching the house. I had no desire to remain there overnight either. The man called Billy may have seen my car, and by now he would have realized that there may be a witness to murder somewhere in or near the vicinity of the old farmhouse. He'd be back, that much was for sure. If he knew that the suitcase was hidden on the premises, he'd be back.

I retrieved my tools from the attic, locked them in the trunk of the rental and got behind the wheel. Fifteen minutes later I was back on the interstate, heading back towards Peoria airport.

CHAPTER 6

I found a Quality Inn near the airport, got a room, showered and went to their eatery for supper. Without thinking, I ordered pork chops. It was all I could do to force down a few bites of my meal and chase it down with water. I asked for my check, signed it with my name and room number, and found the bar.

I sat at the bar until midnight, drinking Jack Daniels and watching an old movie on TV. Actually I half watched the movie. It was George Peppard in "P.J.", one of my favorite PI movies, but my mind was elsewhere. I was thinking of the job I still had to do, the terrible scene I had witnessed, and whether I should just pack it all in and return to LA and tell Rod Sanders to shove his suitcase. Then common sense and the desire to pay some bills and keep my agency afloat got the better of me. I tipped the lady bartender and staggered back to my room, locked the door and went to bed.

I dreamed I was in a pen with a rampaging herd of wild pigs. They were charging at me and I was frantically crawling, trying to get out of the fenced pen before they reached me. Dreams are sometimes prone to abstract thoughts, in my dreams I was trying to figure what a bunch of pigs in a group were called. I woke up in a cold sweat, glanced at the clock on the nightstand and saw that it was only 2 a.m. I didn't feel very good, the effects of the Jack Daniels was working on me. I was a bit dizzy and felt like I might throw up, so I got up and made it to the bathroom where I washed my face in cold water and took tentative sips of water. My stomach felt a little better. I sat in the overstuffed chair and flicked on the TV.

An old Vincent Price movie was on. I clicked through the channels trying to see if anything caught my eye. My mind was racing around in my skull, thinking of crazy things. It occurred to me then that a bunch of pigs in a group is called a herd. I thought of phrases that had the word "pig" in them. "In a Pig's Eye", "Pig in the Poke", "Piggy Bank", finally settling on "Porky Pig" and , half asleep, envisioned Elmer Fudd with a shotgun shooting at poor Porky, who was running towards a barn with other pigs in it, yelling, "h--h-h-help".

I don't know how long I sat there, asleep. My hand slipped off of the arm of the chair and I woke up. I turned the TV off and climbed back in bed. This time I slept without dreaming.

I seldom ask for wake-up calls and rarely use an alarm. I have a built in sixth sense that lets me wake up at a designated time. This morning, however, I overslept. I woke up at 8:30. The sun was already up and when I opened the drapes on the room window, it nearly blinded me. I hastily closed them again, climbed in the shower and let the hot water pour on me, hoping against hope that it would bring me to my senses and that I would decide to say, like Porky Pig says in the movies, "Th-th-th-thats All Folks!" and get back on a plane LA bound.

That didn't happen. I had two cups of coffee from the make it yourself pot in the room, dressed myself in Levis and a polo shirt, pulled on some old Nike running shoes and packed my carry-on bag and tools back to the rental car.

It was nearing noon when I parked the rental in the same spot I had left it the day before. I sat in the car for a few minutes with the windows down, bearing the heat but listening. I heard no sounds that would indicate presence of human beings on the premises. I rolled the window up, got my tools and headed for the house. With any luck I'd have the suitcase and be on a 2 o'clock flight back to L.A.

Everything was just as I had left it. I managed to get my tools and my 175 pounds back in the attic, stepped carefully on the 2 by 4's towards the front and then to my right. I clicked on the battery powered saws-all tool and within a minute I had an opening big enough to step through. Between that partition and the attic roof was another dry wall boarded area. I used the saw and ripped through it in a hurry. According to Sanders I should be able to pick up the suitcase, its weight should not be a problem.

The problem was, there was no suitcase there. I looked left and right in the opening, to make sure I had ripped the right area. No suitcase. I backed out and used the saw to open a larger area to my right, almost half the distance across the attic from front to rear. Again I found dry wall between attic roof and me. I sawed through that and stuck my head in and looked. Nothing.

Either someone had beat me to it, maybe Billy, or the suitcase had been hidden somewhere other than where Rod Sanders thought it was hidden. Just to make sure that there had not been a mistake in Sander's memory cells, I performed basically the same saw and search method on the wall on the other side of the attic. There was no suitcase to be found.

Satisfied that I had searched the attic thoroughly, I dropped the tool bag with the saw in it to the table and then let myself down out of the attic. I was sweating like a stuck hog (pardon the pun) and was thirsty. I found another bottle of water in the refrigerator and drank it.

I sat at the table in silence and thought about what I had accomplished. Maybe the suitcase was somewhere else in the house. I didn't feel like cutting holes in the drywall of every room in the house, but didn't think a precursory search of the rooms would hurt my pride or wear me out. I started with the kitchen and searched every inch. There wasn't much left in the cupboards, a half a box of Cheerios that the mice had chewed through, leaving cereal spread across the shelf. A few cans of vegetables, a can of Franco American spaghetti, and some baby formula.

I wasn't wearing gloves and it dawned on me that if anyone ever found a trace of Cory in the pig yard, my prints were all over the place. I was in no mood to climb back in the attic to wipe away fingerprints, or particularly to worry about fingerprints anyway, so I went to the living room and continued my search. I turned over the dilapidated couch and felt in its sides and back for hidden objects. I found an old pocket knife and a ring of keys, but nothing that I could tie to a suitcase. The key ring did not have a key that I thought came with a set of luggage. I pocketed my find and dropped the couch.

I pried the old shag carpet loose in a corner and lifted it, pulling. It came off of the tacked strip with a ripping sound and I folded it as I pulled until I had it completely up from the floor. Nothing of interest there.

I went on to a bedroom. It had a cheap dresser against a wall, no bed. I opened all the drawers. They were empty. I removed the mirror and looked behind it. Nothing. I turned the drawers upside down and looked on the bottoms. Nothing there. The closet held an old pair of Nike tennis shoes, a pair of child's pajamas, and nothing else. A look in the toe of the shoes revealed nothing but spider webs. In a bathroom, I found a medicine cabinet with a few items. A bottle of pills with a prescription. I dropped it in my pocket. A tube of toothpaste, a toothbrush and a half a bottle of Mennen after shave lotion. No razor, no shaving cream. I took the screws out of the inside of the medicine cabinet and pulled it away from the wall. Nothing. Whoever had been living in the house had packed in a hurry.

The other bedroom was completely empty, no furniture at all, no carpet. A closet held a few clothes hangers but otherwise was empty. Satisfied that I had searched the place well enough to find anything purposefully hidden, not just left behind, I headed for the barn, watching carefully to make sure there were no loose pigs around. One end of the barn was enclosed with large swinging doors, a smaller door was on the side. I entered through the small door and was surprised to find that it was ten degrees cooler in the barn. I listened for a few seconds but heard nothing.

The floor of the barn was concrete. Across from me was a wall with a tool bench, another bench with a drill press and compound saw sat next to it.

I searched the drawers in the tool bench and found nothing but tools of all kinds, and a conglomerate of nuts, bolts and washers. I knelt and looked under the bench and found nothing. I stepped to the end and put both hands under the bench and half lifted, half drug it away from the wall to look behind it. Nothing there.

A wide stairway went up to a loft in the barn. I climbed the stairs carefully and stuck my head above the floor of the loft and had a quick look. I saw nothing but a few bales of straw and an old bicycle. I checked behind the straw and found nothing of interest.

OK, Yardley, I told myself, it's time to cut your losses and get the hell out of Dodge. There's no suitcase here worth fifty grand.

I stopped at a fast food joint and had lunch before heading to the airport.

CHAPTER 7

The flight arrived in LA at 1:30 a.m. I took the shuttle to my car and drove back to my apartment in Santa Monica. It was just as I had left it. Before opening the door I checked the one inch strip of scotch tape I had left in the upper right hand corner, taped from door to frame. It was in place. I'd been bonked severely once by a guy waiting inside my door and since then have developed a habit of using the scotch tape as an indicator whether someone has opened the door or not. It's cheaper than a burglar alarm.

At 11 a.m. I was in Rod Sander's shop.

"There wasn't a suitcase where you said it would be."

"But that's crazy!" He said. "I'm the only person in the world who knew it was there, and it should have been there! I put it there myself!"

"Shoulda, woulda, coulda," I said. "It wasn't there. I ripped out the drywall in the attic and it revealed no suitcase. I checked the rest of the house and the barn. No suitcase."

I did not tell Sanders about the ghastly scene I had witnessed.

"You're not holding out on me, Yardley?" he said.

I came close to smacking a handicapped man across the chops.

"You hired me to do a job. My daddy always told me that if you work for someone, you do the best job you are capable of doing. That's what I did. Now give me my five g's and I'll be on my way."

He sat there, still in a state of disbelief.

A grim, determined look spread across his face and he leaned forward in his wheelchair and looked up at me.

"I'll pay you," he said. "But if I ever find out that you are holding out on me, I'll make you pay, and I will guarantee it will not be pleasant."

"Don't threaten me, Sanders." I growled. "I don't like threats and I don't like being accused of anything I've not done. Either give me my check or the next time you find yourself under water with a wheel chair around your neck may be today."

He opened his desk drawer and got a check ledger. I watched as he made out the check, his face scowling.

I took his check and left.

***

Special Investigator Toby Smith, California Highway Patrol, was in his office. As usual, he was on the phone and two more phones were ringing. He glanced up at me and motioned for me to sit down, held one finger up and then cupped the phone behind his ear and wrote something on his desk blotter.

When he put the phone on its hook he punched a button and said, "Hold my calls," and pushed his chair away from his desk and leaned back.

"What's on your mind, Kip?"

"Can this be an off the record chat?" I asked.

"Sure," he said. "As long as it doesn't implicate you in a crime. If you confess a crime or say anything that implicates you, I'm bound to make it part of the record."

Same old Toby, all business. I'd known him since college days. He'd ran for president of the associated men's student body, with me as his VP. I was elected and he wasn't. I'm not sure if that created a gaff in our friendship then, but if it did, he never let it show. His hairline had receded until his head shined like a new dollar. We're getting old, I told myself.

"I'd like you to watch something I recorded on my cell phone," I said, handing him the phone. "Just push play."

47

"I'm technology oriented, Kip." He said. "I can figure out how to play a movie on a cell phone!"

After a minute of watching he stood up suddenly and scooted the phone across to me.

"Holy crap." He said

"That's what I said," I said.

"Where the hell did you witness that? And why haven't you told the authorities about it? I've got to make this an "on record" report."

"I'm not implicated in committing this crime," I said. "All I did was witness it."

"But a man was shot and fed to the pigs!"

"It is tied to a case I worked," I said. "And it may still be something that I want to investigate, particularly if it can get the fifty grand I was supposed to get."

"Supposed to get?"

I told him the whole story, starting with the party where Sanders got bumped in the pool and ending with Sanders' threat.

He listened intently, walking around his office with his hands behind his back.

When I finished, he stopped pacing and sat down.

"And you want me to do what with this information?"

"Nothing," I said. "At least for a while."

"You know I could lose my job if I don't report this to the Illinois authorities?"

"And I could lose fifty grand if I ever find that suitcase. My contract with Sanders has a "keep it quiet, stupid" clause in it."

"This is some very serious stuff, though, Kip!"

"How did you become aware of it?" I asked. "If anyone says I showed it to you, I'll deny it. Your job isn't in any danger, but my life may be if the wrong people see this. I need that fifty grand. My contract with Sanders is not limited by an expiration date, if I find that suitcase and return it to him, he owes me fifty g's, less the five he paid me."

"I think you're making a mistake," he said. "Looking for that suitcase is like looking for Blackbeard's treasure in Texas. The odds of you finding it are slim and none."

"Maybe," I said. "I've spent a lot of money in the past month trying to get my agency into the big time. That bit in Miami didn't pay a cent. Finding that $114 million lotto ticket was like finding Blackbeard's treasure, but it was Tami's decision to burn it. And I think she did the right thing."

I was referring to the last case I had been involved in, solving a murder and finding a missing Florida Power Vault lotto ticket in the Everglades. The entire case had cost a lovely lady her life. My friend, Tami, had decided the money was blood money and burned the $114 million dollar lotto ticket. It was corrupted from the beginning anyway, and I supported her decision. Toby was familiar with the details.

"If I can find that suitcase and collect the 50g, I can keep the agency going another six months or so until something else breaks. If not, I'm going to have to downsize and a lot of people will be without paychecks, including me."

"Being without a paycheck isn't the worst thing that could happen to you, Old Buddy," he said. "Being eaten by pigs would be worse."

"That's a chance I'll have to take," I said, putting my cell phone in my pocket and standing up. "You do what you have to do, Toby," I said.

"Aw, hell, Kip. You know I'm not going to follow up on this. Not till you tell me it's OK to do so."

"Thanks," I said. "Does that mean I can count on you if I need some help?"

"Get the hell out of my office," he said.

I left. But as I closed his office door I glanced back and saw that he had a faint smile on his face and I knew that our friendship would prevail.

CHAPTER 8

When I want to think about something I have a few places I like to be. One of them is at the beach, and that is where I headed. For a while I had lived in an apartment in Westchester and the nearest beach is El Segundo. There's not a lot of people there usually, no swings for kids, no hot dog stands. Two lifeguard towers and a block building with toilets on either end, one for men, one for women. An eight foot wide cement sidewalk crawls windingly through the sand next to a low wall and small parking lot. The azure blue skies and blue green water reflecting a few paper white clouds was good for me. I was dressed in shorts and tee shirt when I left to go to Sander's office, and that was perfect attire for the beach.

I kicked off my shoes, and walked through the burning sand towards water's edge. The sand was cool where the water surged, and that's where I stopped. I sat down on dry sand just close enough so the waves lapped the water to my toes.

I watched a sailboat cruising a half a mile or so from the shoreline and my mind immediately started to relax. OK, Yardley, I thought, what's next? Where do you start?

I have taken some courses in logic at one point in my career and logical thought progression is a valuable tool. You start by identifying the problem, then logically try to find the cause of the problem before you seek a solution. My problem was the suitcase. What is the cause? It is valuable. Why is it valuable? Something in it is worth a lot of money. What is in it? Ah...that was where logic started to click.

The contents would be a place to start my search to find the missing suitcase. I started by digging into things that might be in a suitcase. My first thoughts were incriminating evidence of a crime, land deeds or property records that might be worth a fortune, a map that would lead to buried or hidden treasure. Eventually I arrived at the obvious and berated myself for wasting time without seeing the obvious. Cash. Good old American money. Moolah. Bread. The Bacon. Lots of it. But where would a guy like Sanders get a suitcase full of cash. I had been told that "he put it there himself." If he put it there, then it followed that whatever was in the suitcase was put in it by Sanders or that he knew the contents.

How much cash can be stuffed in a suitcase? Depends on the size of the suitcase and the denomination of the bills, I figured. Sanders had described the suitcase as a man's large Samsonite and told me it was light enough to carry. He had even attached a picture of it to the contract.

So if the suitcase was full of cash worth enough to pay me $50,000, where did he get that much cash? I knew very little about Sanders except that he had been a big football star. I figured it was time to start doing a little more digging. I walked back to the parking lot and put my socks and shoes on over sandy feet.

I got back in the Caddy and headed for the Redondo Beach library. It is a beautiful old building that sets right near the ocean in Redondo Beach. I'd taken my kids there many times when we lived in the area. It took me twenty minutes to drive from El Segundo to Redondo Beach along the ocean.

The library was nearly empty. I checked in and was assigned a computer at a long table full of computers. The only other person at the table was an old man with long hair that he wore in a pony tail, a rubber band holding it together at his scalp line.

He looked at me and went back to his computer screen. I logged in with the keyword that the librarian had given me and was soon browsing Samsonite suitcases. The site that I was on did not show one even remotely similar to the picture that I remembered from the contract, all of them were newer, plastic. I switched to E-bay and typed in "vintage Samsonite" on the search bar. Two clicks later I was reading the specs.

The picture was a dead ringer for the one provided by Sanders to identify the suitcase on the contract. It was 3 feet long, 1 foot deep and 2 feet wide. How many twenty dollar bills would fit in a suitcase that size? I did a Google search and discovered that all American currency bills are the same dimensions, and that 9600 bills will fit in one cubic foot of space. Rapid math told me that 57,600 bills would fit in the suitcase. If they were all 20's that would be 1,152,000 dollars. I found another site that said one million dollars in 100 dollar bills would weigh 22 pounds. If the suitcase was full of 20's it would weigh 5 times as much or about 110 pounds. Sanders said the suitcase could be picked up easily. Fifty dollar bills would make it weigh about 55 pounds.

If the suitcase was full of fifty dollar bills there would be 2, 880,000 dollars in it.

I whistled loud enough to get a stern look from the librarian. The guy in the ponytail glared at me and I glared back, he quickly looked away.

Where would Sanders get his hands on that kind of money? If he had sold real estate that he owned, escrow would have transferred funds to a bank somewhere and he would have had to withdraw it in cash money. Bearer bonds would be another option, and maybe that was what was in the suitcase.

I went back to Google and typed "unsolved heists" in the search column. I got a list of robberies a lot longer than I would have imagined. On second thought, I added "in Illinois" after "unsolved heists". It took less than five seconds to list them, but the list went all the way back to the early 1800's. I retyped the search. "Unsolved heists in Illinois 1960 to 2010".

The one that showed the most promise was the robbery of a drug company's warehouse by a gang of thieves who cut through the roof and made off with nearly 40 million dollars worth of drugs by backing 40 ft trailers to the dock, loading them with the warehouse forklift, and calmly driving away.

The heist had happened in 2002. They had never been caught. The article stated that the prescription drugs were divided into categories, 1. Pain Killers. 2. Birth Control. 3. Psychological Medicine 4. Heart Medicine and lastly 5. Arthritis Control anti-inflammatory drugs.

The pharmaceutical company was AngiCal-Garner, a Chicago based firm that both manufactured and distributed the drugs. Police estimated that nearly 50 percent of the drugs could be sold on the street within weeks at a value of 20 to 30 million dollars. Then the kicker soaked through my eyes to my brain: *Peoria was the site of the warehouse.*

It wasn't much, but it was a place to start. I decided to fly back to Peoria again and do a little snooping. If I stayed there a week and didn't come up with anything solid, I'd put that part of my investigation on a shelf and try something else, or forget all about the suitcase and Rod Sanders.

CHAPTER 9

A week later I was checked in at the same motel where I had stayed the night after watching a man get eaten alive by pigs. My discomfort over the matter was still lingering, but not nearly as strong as the day it had happened. Something in the day to day processes of being a Private Eye will harden a man. In the week that had transpired since my day in the library, I had worked a case of a missing teen that turned up dead, her body stuffed in a culvert in West LA. I wasn't paid for that one, the police actually found the body and the killer, so all I got was a small retainer. The details of the case were gory enough to make me almost forget the pig incident.

The very next day I was involved in a case where a man was shot by his lover because he refused to divorce his wife and marry her. His wife had hired my firm to find him after he did not come home for three days. It wasn't hard to find him, his lover had stuffed his body in the trunk of her car intending to dump it in the desert, but hadn't got around to it. When I got to the neighborhood to ask questions, I learned about the odor. Neighbors complained about a smell. I called the cops and they found the body.

I got paid for that one, but it wasn't anywhere near the $45,000 I still had coming if I found the elusive suitcase and returned it to Rod Sanders.

So I had misgivings about this case. Something just didn't seem right to me, but since I couldn't put my finger on it, I decided that I would follow up on what little information I had available to me.

All of that was running through my mind as I sat watching TV at the early hour of 7 p.m. the day I arrived back in Peoria. Three hours later I turned off the TV and went to sleep.

I had made a few notes on where I wanted to start the following day, but that could wait. I called my office and told them where I was, left word for one of the guys to take charge of the office until I returned. Then I called Rhonda and made small talk. We had resumed our friendship after my trip to Florida, but things just didn't seem the same to me. I guess it just wasn't in my genes to get married again and start another family. Rhonda was 25 years my junior and still wanted kids and PTA meetings. That part of my life was way too far in the past to ever return.

Early the next morning I was up and raring to get started. I looked at my notes and found that I had not itemized them in the order in which I thought would be best to start. First entry on the list was to find the man who had fed a human being to the pigs. All I had to go on was his first name, and that was Billy.

As usual, something will nag me until I eventually think of it, and such was the case. I remembered the prescription medicine I had found in the medicine cabinet of the house where the suitcase should have been. I searched through my luggage for it but it wasn't there. I played back the images in my mind of the night I had returned home. As is my habit, I had taken everything out of my pockets and put it on my dresser. I remembered putting the container on the dresser. That's probably where it still is, I told myself.

I thought about calling my office and asking someone to go to my apartment and give me the information from the prescription container, but it was early in Peoria, only 7 a.m. so it would be 5 a.m. in LA and no-one would be at the office yet. I glanced at my list again and read the second entry. "Check on the license plate of the car that was in the driveway of the house."

I flipped open my laptop and did a Google search on the property address as I had before my first trip to Peoria. It didn't take long to find, and I did a screen print on the picture, opened the file in

Windows Viewer and zoomed in on the area of the license plate. It was an Illinois plate. I copied the information and decided that a trip to a local DMV might be the place to start.

I ate a healthy breakfast in the motel restaurant and making sure I had all of the information I would need, including my California PI license, wallet, and gun, I climbed into the rented Chevy and headed for the Illinois Department of Vehicle Registration office. Peoria has five offices within a 30 mile radius of downtown. I headed for the one on the south side, located in the village of Pekin.

My search had told me that the offices are not open until 8 a.m. but what I failed to notice was the fact that none of the offices are open on Mondays, just Tuesday through Saturday. Since this was Monday morning, it was totally surprising to me when I arrived at the office at 8:20, there was not a car in the lot. I entered the lot and parked the Chevy and sat there thinking. Almost immediately I realized that the place was closed. I opened my laptop and did the search again and confirmed my thoughts. Almost an hour wasted and I was cursing my lack of observation.

I called Rhonda. I knew she would be up at that hour, and since she had a key to my place, she might be willing to help me with the prescription bottle idea.

"Hello," she answered, on the second ring.

"Good morning, beautiful," I said.

"Kip?"

"Live and in living color, beautiful," I said. "I'm sorry if I woke you."

"I'm up," she said. "I'm just surprised to hear from you. Where are you?"

"Peoria, Illinois," I said. "I just need a small favor, if you can do it, I'll be eternally indebted to you."

"You're already eternally indebted to me, Kip Yardley," she said. "I've got a backlog of favors I've done for you. Someday I hope to call in a few markers."

"I'll be glad to start on that task as soon as I get home, beautiful."

"OK, Kip." She said. "What can I help you with this morning?"

"Will you go over to my place and look on my dresser for a prescription bottle, and call me with the information?"

"Is something wrong? Have you got a cold or headache or something? Is your back bothering you again?"

"No, it's not for me," I said. "It's part of a case I'm on. Will you do it?"

"Well, I'm glad you aren't sick," she said. "OK, Kip. What time do you want me to call you? As soon as I've got the information?"

"Yes, please," I said. "You're a Doll."

"It'll probably be about 9 LA time, I haven't even showered yet."

"No problem. Just call me when you get it, OK?"

"OK, Kip. Love you." She said.

"I love you too, Doll," I said.

She hung up and I felt a twinge of guilt. She was right. I owed her a lot more than I could ever pay. I knew that she was still thinking of the "M" word, and I was thinking more of the "S" word. Marriage versus Sex. She wanted one with the other, I wanted one without the other.

Two and a half hours to kill. I glanced at the notes again. Number three on the non-prioritized list was:

"Check with pharmaceutical company regards heist."

Angi-Cal-Garner distribution center was on Peoria's south side, near the airport. I headed back in that direction, found the street off of Interstate 74, just by luck, and drove into their parking lot. Directions on a sign told me how to find employment one way, receptionist another, and general offices a third. The sidewalk to "general offices" was barred by an electronic gate. I opened the door marked "receptionist" and entered.

The woman at the desk was in her forties, light hair pulled back into a neat pony-tail, nicely dressed. She looked like Beaver Cleaver's mom.

"Can I help you, Sir?" She asked.

"Perhaps," I said, smiling. "I'm an Investigative Reporter doing a story on unsolved crimes for a book I'm writing. I'd like to talk to someone about the unsolved heist here back in 2002."

"Oh, that's before my time," she said. "I'll get Mr. Dudley for you."

She pushed a button, glanced up and smiled at me.

"He's been here the longest, he may remember details," she said.

"Mr. Dudley? I have a gentlemen here that wishes to speak to someone regarding the loss in 2002."

She glanced at me again. "I'm sorry, what did you say your name is?"

"I didn't say," I said. "Please tell him I'll explain my call if he'll see me."

She relayed my request.

"Yes, sir," she said into the mouthpiece. "I'll send him right in."

She showed me through the main door and told me she would buzz me through the electronic gate and to take the second office on the left.

I followed her instructions, pushing the gate when it buzzed and opening the second door on my left.

Mr. Dudley's office was protected in the front by a secretary's desk, but no secretary. A six foot divider behind the desk was in my view, but I saw the head and shoulders of a man behind it.

Dudley was well over six feet tall.

"What can I help you with, I'm Cass Dudley."

"Hello, Mr. Dudley," I said. "I'm Kip Yardley, an Investigator from LA. I'm trying to do some research on the drug heist that occurred here a few years ago. My client is writing a book about Southern Illinois and has hired me to ask some questions."

"What kind of questions? I've been over that with the police at least a dozen times."

"I won't take much of your time, sir." I said. "May I come in?" I was already "in" but I wanted to sit down and talk to Dudley, not over the top of a divider.

"OK."

I walked through an aisle opening and around the divider. His desk was covered with paperwork.

I would guess that his age was near 55, he was starting to bald and lines under his eyes made his narrow face look tired.

"Thank you, sir." I said. "May I sit down?"

"OK"

I sat.

"Mr. Dudley, I understand you were employed here at the time of the heist?"

"Yes."

"Can you tell me what your position was at that time, and what you remember about that night?"

"Well, I was in charge of shipping and receiving then," he said. "I'm General Manager in charge of operations now."

"Yes, sir." I said.

"I was at home when I got a call from the police telling me that one of my employees had showed up for work to find the doors open and two of our 40 foot trailers missing, along with about 95 percent of our inventory."

"The thieves took two of your trailers?" That was information I didn't remember from the library story.

"Yes. They brought their own tractors, hooked up to two of our empty trailers, backed them up to the dock and loaded them with $12 million dollars of inventory and drove away."

"How did they get in to the premises?"

"Cut a hole in the roof with a chain saw, came down on a rope and opened the bay doors."

"The bay doors were electrically operated?"

"Yes."

"No locks on the controls for the doors?"

"No."

"I understand you are a distribution center. Did you advertise the purpose of the building? In other words, how did the thieves know you stored prescription drugs?"

"No, we didn't advertise. Our company name is outside on the sign, but that's all."

"Who was the General Manager when that happened? Is he still with the company?"

"That would have been Marion Ford. He left shortly afterward. I think he was fired, but I don't know for sure."

"Any idea where he went?"

"No."

I stopped for a minute. Usually when a big shot leaves a company there are rumors flying around about where he went, particularly when the same rumors report that he has been terminated.

"Did you think it was strange that no rumors surfaced about where Mr. Ford found employment?"

"Didn't think of it," he said.

"Is that when you were promoted to GM?"

"No. The assistant GM was moved up. He stayed on for about six months, then resigned."

"Can you tell me his name?"

"Ransom. I believe his first name was Richard, but he went by R.D. Ransom. No-one ever used his first name, just initials."

"Do you have a list of all the employees who were on staff at that time?"

"Well, I'd have to look. I think there's a bunch of old company phone books around somewhere. I might be able to find one from that time frame."

"Would you mind doing that?"

"I'm pretty busy, Mr. Yardley."

"Thank you for your time," I said. "If I think of anything else, may I call you?"

"Sure."

"Oh, there is one more thing. Were the trailers ever found?"

"That's a funny thing," he said. "We never saw them again. Had to buy two more."

"Who manufactures those trailers? Are they local?"

"We bought them from a dealer here in Peoria," he said. "Fruehauf, I think makes them. Denton Trailers is the dealer."

"Thanks again," I said.

I stood up and shook his hand.

He shook hands with a loose, limp grip, like my hand was dirty or alien to him.

I left his office and returned the way I had entered until I found the receptionist.

"Sorry to bother you again," I said, " just wanted to say thanks. Oh by the way, Mr. Dudley mentioned some old company phonc books and that there may be one from thc timc framc of the heist. Would you happen to know where those books are?"

"I could look," she said

I opened my wallet and took out a twenty.

"I'd give $20 for one, if you can find them," I said.

"Let me look," she said.

She left the cubicle and was gone a few minutes. I stood looking at pictures on the wall. They were mostly of people, a few in suits and ties but a lot of them were dressed semi-casual. No names, just people.

When she returned she was carrying two old company phone books.

"I found one from the year before and one from the year after," she said, extending them to me.

I took them and extended the twenty.

"Oh that's not necessary," she said. But she took the twenty.

"Thank you very much, you've been very helpful."

I left.

CHAPTER 10

At eleven Peoria time Rhonda called me. "I've got the information from the bottle, Kip."

"Let me get a pencil, Babe," I said. I flipped open my briefcase, grabbed a pencil and my notebook. I have a habit of keeping a notebook on every case I work, writing down things so I don't forget them, and jotting down inconsequential items sometimes that I can refer back to if needed.

"OK" I said.

"It was issued to Cindy Brooks. It is for pain."

"Give me the prescribing physician's name, please."

"Doctor McMann," she said. "Do you want his phone number and address?"

"Yes please."

She rattled them off and I jotted them down in the book. I knew that I'd be fighting a Doctor-Patient confidentiality factor but I thought it might be worth a try to get some information from the Doctor.

"Thanks, Rhonda," I said. "I owe you one."

"I'll be waiting to collect."

We said our goodbyes and I did a Google search on the address she had given me. It showed the office of the Doctor on Main street, right in the heart of Peoria. I decided to make that my next item on my "to do" list and headed the rented car in the direction of the interstate that would lead me to the downtown area. I thought of calling, but it has been my experience that phone calls can sometimes be a waste of time instead of cutting time. Particularly if I can talk one on one to a receptionist or someone and convince them of my "need to know" on the information I am requesting.

And such was the case.

Doctor Mann's receptionist was a girl just past her teens, pretty and talkative. She wore a very large engagement ring on her left hand and I used that to try to loosen her up for my questions.

"Wow. Congratulations!" I said.

She smiled at me and glanced at the ring.

"Thank you."

"When's the big day?" I asked, trying to sound as if I was really interested.

"Oh not for a while yet," she said. "I wanted a fall wedding, but Ricky wants to get married in June and honeymoon in Antigua."

"Nice," I said.

"Can I help you, sir? The Doctor isn't in yet, but will be in an hour. Do you need to make an appointment?"

"No, I am actually seeking some information. My name is Kip. I'm with the Los Angeles investigation team." I opened my wallet and showed her my badge briefly and closed it. Sometimes it works, sometimes it doesn't. This time it did.

"We are always willing to co-operate with the police," she said. I knew this would be easier than I had imagined.

"I just need an address for one of your patients. Cindy Brooks? She may be involved in a prescription medicine ring we are investigating." I lied with a straight face. I'd been telling untruths during investigations for so long that I was getting good at it. Every investigator I know, including cops, will lie like crazy to get information that might help with their case. It's even legal for police to lie to suspects during criminal interrogation.

She clicked and tapped a computer.

"She lives at ..oh, wait a second. She's moved. Let me see if we have her new address. It isn't on the computer."

She opened a drawer and pulled out a log book, like one you would use to keep track of horse betting or scores at the golf course.

"Cindy, Brooks...Barrister, Barnett, Broman, oh here it is, Brooks, Cindy."

She gave me the address and I wrote it down in my own log book.

"Would you mind giving me her previous address?" I asked. "Just to make sure that we are talking about the same person?"

She opened the computer again and gave me the address of the farmhouse that I had visited looking for the suitcase. Bingo.

"Do you happen to know her husband's name?" I asked.

"It's William."

Billy!

"William Brooks?" I asked.

"Yes. According to our information, they are separated, though. I'm not sure if they are divorced."

I said a silent thank you for talkative teens and then thanked her for being helpful.

"Congratulations again," I said. "I hope you have a long and happy marriage."

"Why thank you, Sir!" She gushed. "That's nice of you."

"Let me give you my cell phone number," I said. "If Cindy comes back in within a few weeks, please call me." I rattled off my cell phone number and she wrote it down and attached it to the log book page with a paper clip.

I thanked her again and left.

Out in the parking lot I had just opened the door on the rented Chevy when a man approached me moving very fast. Instinctively I turned to face him.

"Stay the hell away from my wife," he said.

"I don't think I know you, buddy," I said.

"You don't need to know me. I'm just warning you, stay away from my wife"

"Sure. Problem is, I don't even know your wife. If I meet her, I'll be glad to stay away from her."

"Don't get funny, asshole," he said.

If there's one thing that I don't like to be called, it is "asshole".

Now my dander started to get up a little.

"You're the one that's funny, buddy. I don't know you, I don't know your wife, so get out of my sight."

"Here's what you'll get if you keep trying to see her, asshole," he said, and threw a right roundhouse punch aimed at my head.

I didn't know him and he sure as hell didn't know me.

I went under the punch and behind him so fast that he probably thought I was a Mexican magician doing a vanishing act. Uno, Dos, vanished without a Tres. From behind him I kicked the back of his left knee and he went down, hitting his head on the door of the Chevy.

I stood back waiting for him to get up.

"Now you're really going to hurt, asshole!" He said.

That's when I kicked him hard in the chest with a front kick. The back of his head bounced off of the Chevy like a Kobe Bryant bank shot.

I stood back again.

"Quit calling me asshole, asshole," I said. "If you do, I'll quit kicking you like a football."

He looked up at me, rolled over on all fours and pushed himself up to a kneeling position. He grabbed the opened door and pulled himself erect, and turned slowly to face me.

"Sorry, I must have made a mistake," he said, with a rasping voice.

"You made more than one mistake," I said. "You called me "asshole" three times. That's three mistakes."

I was still waiting for whatever move he tried to make, feet about even with my shoulders, hands in front of my belly button, fingers curled into fists.

He looked at me sideways and closed the door so that he didn't have to come too close to me, and walked away, limping on the leg I had kicked. I let him walk.

"Stay away from her," he said. "Next time I'll just shoot you."

I didn't reply to that. No need. I'm not an easy person to shoot. I stay extremely alert and I respond very quickly. If you ever plan to shoot me, you'll probably have to do it from 100 yards away, otherwise you might wind up getting shot.

My first thoughts were that he had simply made an identity mistake. Then I started thinking about it. Maybe he was the estranged husband of Cindy Brooks, and not the "Billy" I was looking for. He didn't resemble the Billy that fed a man to hogs. That Billy was stocky, muscular and not over 5 feet 9 inches. This guy was at least 6 feet tall, slender

I got in the car and used my laptop to pull up the address given to me for Cindy Brooks. She lived in an apartment building not far from the downtown area, so I decided to visit her, unannounced, and ask her if she had ever seen a suitcase like the one I was looking for.

Ten minutes later I was knocking on her door.

The woman who answered was attractive. She had a pretty face, surrounded by curly dark hair. A little boy about two hung on to her skirt like she was trying to get away from him.

"Yes?"

"Good morning, Mrs. Brooks?"

"It used to be," she said. "I'm Cindy Stronheim, now."

"Your ex husband was William Brooks?"

"Yes. What is it you want?"

"I'd just like to ask a few questions, Mrs. Stronheim," I said. "May I come in? I won't take much of your time."

"Are you a bill collector? If you are, you're out of luck. Ed isn't here and I don't have any money."

"No, I'm an investigator," I said, and showed her my PI badge. She glanced at it and I put it away.

"Come in," she said, and I went inside. The small apartment was furnished sparsely, furniture that might have came from Goodwill or The Salvation Army. I glanced around. It was clean, but there was a pile of dirty clothes in the middle of the floor.

"Don't mind my wash," she said. "I've got to get these down to the laundry room."

I stepped around the pile of clothes and sat down on a stiff backed chair.

"I won't take long," I said again. "You lived out south of town in a farm house not long ago?"

"Yes. That is when I was married to Billy."

"Billy Brooks?"

"Yes."

"Did you ever see a large leather suitcase, a Samsonite, while you lived there? Did anyone ever bring one to the house?"

"A suitcase?" She asked. "No, we didn't even own a suitcase. Every time we moved we used Wal-Mart bags to put our clothes in. Billy went from job to job, never held down a good job. That's one reason I left him."

"While you lived there, did anyone ever do any repair or remodeling in the attic room?"

"No, not to my knowledge," she said. "But I left twice. Once I went to Florida and stayed with my

Mom for about three months. Billy stayed here. He was working for the man who owns the pigs."

That caught my attention.

"Who owns the pigs?"

"An older man named Stevenson. I don't know his first name. Billy took care of the pigs and the man paid him $400 a week. Then one day he came and found two of his pigs nearly dead and the rest half starved. He fired Billy, called him a dead beat, and said he wasn't worth making hog food out of. Another job Billy had but couldn't keep."

"You mean Billy wouldn't feed the pigs?"

"Oh he fed them the first month or so," she said. "Then he got to running around playing poker and drinking, and the pigs didn't get fed. Damned if I was going to do it. I ain't felt right since I lost my older boy."

"Your older child died?"

"Yes," she said. "Billy wouldn't let me take him to the Doctor. He said my sickness was costing him too much money already, so Christopher's illness got worse and worse. One night he just died. I woke up the next morning and he was dead."

She looked away from me towards the kitchen, her eyes glistening with tears.

"Can I offer you some coffee, Mister? What did you say your name is?"

"Yardley, Cindy. Kip Yardley. And I'm very sorry about your boy."

I've known people who have lost children to illnesses when the child was treated by the best doctors money could buy. To think that someone would not try to get medical help for their child because it cost too much, in my way of thinking, was barbaric. If I ever meet with Billy, I intend to remember this moment.

She got up and went to the small kitchen, got two cups and poured coffee in them, returning to the living room. She handed me one and smiled.

"Sorry, I don't have any cream and sugar. I've learned to like it black."

"This is fine," I said. "How long have you been away from that farm house?"

"Since a year ago last month," she said. "I filed for divorce then. Donnie, here, was not quite a year old then."

"Was your ex-husband ever in jail?" I asked.

"How did you know?" she asked me.

"I didn't," I told her. "Just part of my investigation."

"Yes, he spent four years in Joliet," she said. "That was right before we got married. We were engaged when he went in, and got married right after he got out."

"What was his crime?" I asked.

"He took some old truck trailers to Florida," she said. "The police had been looking for the trailers and Billy got stopped for speeding in

Alabama and the police arrested him. Charged him with possession and transporting stolen property across state lines."

Now I was really interested. Billy might have been involved in the drug heist

"So you've been divorced for about a year?" I said, trying not to look surprised or extremely interested in the trailer tale.

"Yes, sir," she said. "I re-married three months ago."

She went to a bedroom and came back with a picture in a dark frame.

"This is my new husband," she said.

I looked. It was the guy who had just warned me to stay away from his wife.

"This is Mr. Stronheim?"

"Yes," she said. "Ed Stronheim. Do you know him?"

"We've met," I said, and let it go at that. "Did Mr. Stronheim know Billy? Particularly before he went to prison?"

"I don't think so," she said. "If he did, he never mentioned it."

"How about Mr. Stronheim's police record, Cindy? Has he ever been in prison?"

"He was in Joliet too," she said. "But he's being very good, he's got a good job and goes to work every day. He is past his parole, doesn't have to report anymore. We're getting better, Mr. Yardley, both of us."

"Both of you?" I said. "Have you been in prison too?"

"No," she said. "But I have had a problem. I used drugs. I've been clean now for three years. So we are trying hard." She turned her head away from me again, and I could once more see the film of tears suddenly appear. I wanted to hold her and comfort her. But then I had work to do, and the world is full of people who need comforting. Time doesn't permit me to extend comfort to all of them.

"Thank you, Cindy," I said. "You've been a big help."

"I have?"

"Yes, and thanks," I said.

CHAPTER 11

I drove to a fast food place and had lunch, ate slowly, trying to digest not only the food, but what I had learned so far. I had few leads left and was beginning to think I'd made a mistake coming back to Peoria to try to get a clue and track down that damned suitcase. But then, fifty grand is fifty grand.

I called my old buddy, Toby.

"What is it now?" He asked as soon as my call went to his office phone.

"Toby, old pal, old buddy," I said.

"Come on, Kip. Get it over with. I know you want something of me, that's about the only time you call any more. I've got Lakers tickets that are burning a hole in my pocket, and your off chasing wild pigs somewhere."

"As a matter of fact, I do need a small favor," I said.

"And just what would that be, and how small is it?"

"I need an intro to the unsolved cases officer here. Can you set that up for me?"

"I'll call you back in five minutes," he said. "If you don't answer, I'll know you went to shit and the hogs ate you."

"Funny," I said. He hung up.

It was more like ten minutes later, but he called me.

"See a man named Fritz Donahue at the main station in Peoria." He said.

"Thanks, Toby," I said. "I owe you one."

"One is a lonely number, Kip. You owe me so damned many I don't have enough time left to collect."

I hung up on him.

The downtown area of Peoria is really not all that bad. The buildings are old. The courthouse is an old building, 4 stories tall, looks like the typical official building of the time. Peoria was named after the Peoria tribe, prevalent in the area when Louis and Clark explored up the Illinois River from the Mississippi. The first settlement was simply called Fort Clark but when that structure burned and was rebuilt, the town name became Peoria.

I paid to park in a city lot and walked to the Police Department in the courthouse building. A curly haired young lady pointed me down a hallway towards a cubicle that had a black plastic sign at the top, "Fritz Donahue, Cold Cases". Someone had pasted a plastic strip under the sign that read, "Do not enter unless you've got one. Bud preferred."

I stopped at the door. A big, brawny guy in a short sleeved white shirt sat with his back to me, his desk covered with folders.

"Mr. Donahue?"

He spun around in his swivel chair and looked at me over the top of thin reading glasses.

"What kind you got?"

"I beg your pardon?"

"The sign," he said. "Bud gets you ten minutes. Anything else gets you five unless its Coors Lite. That horse piss will get you knocked on your ass."

"Oh," I said. He looked like he meant it, that was the bad part.

"Well?"

"Toby Smith from California CHP Special Investigations told me to ask for you."

"Oh yeah. Come on in. You can buy me a case later. Bud, of course."

I went in.

"Have a seat," he said, pulling out an old wooden straight backed chair and spinning it around to face his.

I offered my hand to shake, and he danged near broke it.

"Nice meetin' ya."

I sat down.

"What's on your mind, Pal?" He asked.

"I'm working a case that I believe involves the Pharmaceutical robbery a few years back. Toby said you might be able to help."

"I haven't had anything on that in a long time," he said. "Last bit I had was the trailer driver got busted for speeding in Alabama and the FBI impounded the trailers."

"That's where I'm at," I said. "Did the trailers come back to Peoria?"

"Yeah. We had 'em brought back up. Didn't do any good. The crime lab boys went over them with a fine tooth comb and didn't find a thing. No prints except the ones of the driver that got busted."

"What happened to them after that?" I asked.

"We're still paying storage on them. Someday we may crack that case and we'll need the trailers as evidence. City pays two hundred a month to store them."

"I'd like to see them." I said, even though I had no idea why I thought I could determine anything by looking at two old trailers.

"Sure," he said. "They're at Barnfield transport, out near the bypass. You know where the bypass crosses the interstate?"

"I'm not from around here," I said.

He drug out a yellow legal tablet, scribbled some lines on it, wrote some words on it and handed it to me. It was a rough drawn map with street names and the name "Barnfield" on a big square with an "X" under it.

" X marks the spot," he said. "Dos Equis will get you my life story."

"Do you have a current address on Billy, the guy who went to jail for driving the trailers?"

He made a curling motion with his right hand, "Give it back, I'll jot his address on there," he said.

I gave back the map he had drawn. He opened a folder and read it, pushing the reading glasses up on his nose, then wrote on the yellow sheet and handed it back.

I glanced at it. "Billy Dan Brooks, 1922 St Road 483, Peoria, IL."

I recognized the address as the place where I had seen a man eaten alive by pigs.

"Anything else?" Donahue asked.

"What would it take to get a copy of that file?" I asked, pointing to the folder he had just looked in.

"Can't hurt anything," he said. "Now it's two cases of Bud."

He got up and walked out of his cubicle to a copy machine on the opposite wall of the office. He stood there copying pages while I looked around. There were pictures on the inside walls of his work space. Some of them were homicide shots, some were just people. Several were pictures of a softball team in various degrees of play or posing with trophies. Across the jerseys of the uniformed players were two words, "Peoria Buds".

I made a mental note to get a couple of cases of longneck Bud delivered to Donahue. Now I knew how Toby got me an interview so fast. Toby is big on slow pitch softball and plays on the California CHP travelling team. They play in Law Enforcement tournaments all around the country. He probably had met and remembered Donahue.

"How do you know Toby?" I asked, when he returned with an inch thick stack of copied papers. He handed them to me and slid the original folder back on his desk.

"Softball." He said. "Met him in LA last year when we kicked the shit out of his team for the Law Enforcement championship."

"Anything I can help you with, call me," he said. "And if you get something you'd better call me first, or I'll find you and kick the shit out of you.

Somehow I believed him.

CHAPTER 12

I took the folder full of information regarding the cold case and found a small park near the center of town where I sat at a concrete picnic table in the shade and went through it At first glance there was nothing that I didn't already know or thought I knew. The details in general were pretty much what I had already learned from newspaper and internet accounts, and my talk with Cass Dudley at Angi-Cal-Garner distribution center. Most of the folder concerned crime scene details that were not of interest to me.

I finished flipping through the folder and got back in the rental car and headed for the transportation depot where the two trailers were stored. I had no idea what I expected to find, if anything, but a bell kept silently dinging in the back of my mind. I've learned to pay attention to those bells. Most of the time they start when my mind is trying to tell me something is important, and not to overlook it. Call it intuition or omen. It has happened so many times that it has become second nature to me to follow up.

A security guard who appeared to be in his seventies, baggy blue pants, a lighter blue shirt with a shiny badge, a gun slung low like a gunfighter out of a B Western movie, showed me through the gates and pointed at a trailer at the end of a long row.

"Last one down there," he said. "Hasn't been moved since they brought it in here, tires are all low. If you're planning on moving it, better bring a compressor. I don't think they've had state inspection for a while either."

I thanked him and walked the graveled area towards the trailers. He was right, there was two trailers there. They looked like two tramps sleeping in military barracks next to all of the shiny new trailers. Neither of the two were locked so I pushed the lever up on the first one, cranked it left and swung the right hand door out. A musty smell escaped from the interior and wafted over me like the smell of wet leaves on a spring day. I looked in and saw nothing but a wooden floor that stretched all the way to the darker interior. I stepped up on the steel brackets that all trailers are required to have. My body complained when I pulled myself up in the trailer. It was a sign that my younger, physically fit and full of piss and vinegar days were on the threshold of old age. I stepped gingerly down the center, not knowing the condition of the wooden floors, or any subfloor beneath them.

I stopped to let my eyes acclimate to the interior dimness, then examined the walls, the floors and every inch that I could see. I didn't know what I was looking for, but whatever it was, I intended to find it.

As the interior light got gradually dimmer, I got a small LED flashlight from my pocket and turned it on, playing it on the walls as I walked. The light from the flashlight reflected off of the aluminum walls. Something caught my eye. The reflection seemed a little brighter as the beam of the light passed over a certain spot on the aluminum. I reversed the direction of the sweep and saw it again. I stepped closer, holding the beam on the spot that had appeared brighter.

I saw where someone had written something with a pencil. It was faint, and almost unnoticeable, but there it was. It said simply, "Mary" and under it was an area that was shinier than the rest. Someone had written something there and then erased it. I stepped closer until my eyes were inches away from the wall. I could see a few black squiggly marks. I looked closer and could tell that once it had been a series of numbers, There was part of an 8 and either a 1 or a 7. Telephone number? I wondered.

Nothing else was visible.

Whatever number had been there had at one time been important to someone. It was also important enough, probably to the same someone, to erase it. My mind thought of the "If you want to have fun, call Mary at 555-1212" messages written by jilted boyfriends in men's stalls across many states. I didn't think this was that type of message. If it was, it would all be there, including the phone number. This message had been written because the writer intended to call the number at some point, or the number was important enough to him to jot down. Once he had the number committed to memory, he rubbed it out. Whoever Mary was probably got a phone call before her phone number was obliterated.

I got out of the trailer and walked back to the Security Guard's shack.

"I've got to get something from my car, be right back," I said.

"Sure," the guard replied. "If I'm asleep, don't wake me." He laughed heartily.

When I had decided to go back to Peoria, I took the canvas bag with the tools that I had taken on the first trip, just in case I decided to go back to the farmhouse and rip out more drywall in search of the suitcase.

Now I carried the heavy bag through the gate, glanced inside the shack and saw the Security Guard sitting at a desk with his feet propped up, reading a newspaper.

Back to the trailer. I took the blade off of the saw and turned it over so that the teeth would rotate in the opposite direction. I hoped the battery had enough charge in it to do the job I wanted to accomplish. I set the bag in the trailer and hoisted myself back up, picked up the bag and walked to the spot where I had seen the writing. I got out the saw and carefully cut a two by two inch square from the aluminum I purposefully left a small spot in the bottom left hand corner of the cut so that the piece wouldn't fall between the interior aluminum and the outer shell. It wasn't difficult, and the saw had enough juice left to finish the job. Then I took my pocket knife and inserted it on the right side of the cut piece and pried out. I cut a little patch of cloth from my tee shirt and held it between my fingers and the aluminum to avoid leaving my prints on it. It took a little wiggling back and forth until the corner broke and I had the square cut of aluminum wrapped in the tee shirt material and put it in my pocket.

I have a friend back in California who is a genius. He has a degree from UCLA in chemical analysis. He's a bit of a weird duck, talks in rhyming sentences half the time and insists that we attend sporting events together. He's helped me on more than one occasion when I had some problem with a clue that I thought was important. I probably owed him more than one Lakers game and a couple of meals, but I was going to see if he could read the rest of the numbers on this piece of aluminum.

I found a Post Office and bought a small box. I pulled Richard Rheames card from my wallet and copied the address on the box, carefully inserted the cloth wrapped aluminum piece, sealed the box and mailed it.

Out in the street I called Richard.

"Richard Rheames, or so it seems," he said when he answered.

"Hi Richard, it's Kip Yardley, Hale and Hearty."

He laughed, a full throated, hearty laugh.

"You're catching on to the way I talk," he said. "It brightens up my day and a lot of people get a kick, private dick."

I laughed at that one.

"Can you do something for me, Richard?" I asked.

"Ask and thou shall receive, hale and hearty, Kip Yardley."

"I'm sending you a small square of aluminum on which someone wrote a number, then erased it. Can you somehow extract the number?"

"Not with the naked eye, guy."

"How about with high powered spectrometry or some such critter?"

He was silent for a few seconds.

"You there?"

"I'm still on the air, Teddy Bear." He said.

"Well?"

"I'll have to see it, Kip. Graphite and aluminum are two different elements. If there was moisture involved, there might have been enough galvanic corrosion to etch the number in the aluminum. When did you mail it?"

"Just did," I said. "I sent it special delivery. They said you'd get it in two business days."

"I'll get on it as soon as a sonnet," he said. I had no idea what that one meant.

'Thanks, Richard," I said. "I owe you one."

"More than one, moron."

I hung up.

CHAPTER 13

Back in the car, I sat for a long time going over things in my mind. I still had some things that I wanted to check out, but everything seemed scrambled.

I had resisted buying a cell phone until it became apparent that if I wanted to communicate with anyone while on a case, I might have to drive a hundred miles around city streets to find a phone booth.

At that point my cell phone rang.

"Kip Yardley."

"Hi Kip, it's Rhonda. How are you?"

"Rhonda! I was just thinking of you."

"Something nice, I hope."

"Always," I said.

"When do you think you'll be coming home, Kip?"

"Not sure, Kid," I said. Kid is a nickname I use for her since way back. It was from an old Humphrey Bogart movie we had watched together once.

"Well, I hope it's soon," she said. "I just called to say "I love you".

"Love you too, Kid." I said.

"Did the prescription information help?"

"I found the lady," I said. "She was willing to talk, but I don't yet know if she has given me any information that is useful or pertinent to the case I'm working on."

"I was hoping you would find her and that she would break the case for you, Kip. I miss you."

"Miss you too," I said. Actually I was missing Rhonda some, but the details of the daily grind, chasing down clues, digging into stuff that might have no meaning or might mean everything, had kept my mind so full that the thought of the long legged Rhonda swimming in her pool with no clothes on had barely, no pun intended, crossed my mind,.

"Call me once in a while," she said. "I love you."

She hung up before I had a chance to say anything further.

Now I was befuddled....confused. Should I just toss all of this in the garbage and go back to LA, work a few "cheating spouse" cases for the Hollywood crowd or try to hang on and take back a suitcase worth 50 grand?

"That is a no brainer, Yardley," I told myself out loud. An old lady, walking her dog along the sidewalk next to my car, looked at me like I was crazy. Her dog growled, then barked. He thought I was crazy, too.

I drove back to the park and sat at the same concrete table and looked through the company directory for Angi-Cal-Garner distribution center. There were a total of 55 people working at the center when the great burglary occurred.

I skimmed down through the list of names rapidly, looked at the employee's picture if the name seemed familiar or rang any bells in my mind. As I had already begun to suspect, Billy Brooks had been employed during that time frame. I studied the picture. It was the same Billy Brooks that had tossed a wounded man to the hogs and watched as the hogs ripped the man to pieces. He had been an order picker at the company.

I let my mind go back to that day. I had been just about ready to start sawing drywall when I heard the first shot. It had taken me a few seconds to get to the front window of the attic.

I took my cell phone out and found the file with the scene as I had filmed it. I compared the picture of the man standing with his hands in the air to the picture I had before me. It was Billy Brooks, all right. No mistake.

As the scene played again on the cell phone, something suddenly caught my attention. It was faint and I could barely hear it, but it was there. "Please, I don't know. Please, Cory, I'd tell you if I knew, You've got to believe me."

I don't know why I hadn't made a connection previously, but the name Cory hung in the air like the whistle of a train on a foggy morning.

I remembered the scene right before Sanders went in the pool the day I got tangled up in this fiasco.

The girl was mocking the big man. He had just told her not to mention someone's name again. She had replied by repeating the name several times.

"Cory, Cory, Cory."

The name is not an unheard of one. I was beginning to wonder if it had any connection. I pulled out my well worn note pad and turned it to the next blank page, took a ball point pen and wrote:

"Check to see if Sanders knew the couple who fought. See if he knows anyone named Cory."

I opened the directory and started at the top again and carefully looked through the list of employees. Near the bottom I found something interesting. Cory West.

I stared at the page.

The guy in the photo was a big man. He might have been considered handsome by some women's standards, despite the fact that his nose had been broken at some point in his life, and lay slightly to the right of center like Brian Williams on the 5:30 news.

He fit the description of the man who had cross words with Sanders, according to Monique.

I used the cell phone to snap a picture of the picture in the directory.

Next I sent a text message to Monique and included the picture. In my message I asked her if the picture was of the person that she had told me about, the one who visited Sanders at his office. The one who had some four letter words to say before the visit ended. If her answer was "yes", I could tear out the last page in my notebook.

Almost immediately my phone buzzed. It was Monique. "That's the man who visited Mr. Sanders at his office." she texted. "Brunch on Sunday?"

"I'm out of town," I sent back. "I'll call when I get back. Thanks."

I looked at the directory picture again. Cory West was an assistant logistics supervisor when employed by the drug distributor. He was shown as 22 years of age, a graduate of Southern Illinois University, married, no children. On a hunch I called the Peoria PD and asked to speak to Fritz Donahue.

The softball playing detective answered almost immediately.

"Donahue."

"Mr. Donahue, this is Kip Yardley. I need to ask a question, then I'll owe you two cases of Bud Lite. "

"This isn't being recorded is it, Yardley? I could go to jail for taking a bribe if it is."

I laughed. "Not a chance. I just want to know if there is a missing person file for a man named Cory West."

The phone was eerily silent for several seconds.

"You there, Donahue?"

"Yeah." He said. "How'd you arrive at that? Remember what I told you about holding back?"

I thought about that for a minute. What should I tell him? I decided to wing it, and not put all my eggs in one basket, at least not yet.

"I can't find him," I said. "It's just standard procedure for me to check with local police departments when I can't find someone. Usually if they are breathing, I can find them, not bragging about my abilities, much."

"How much have you looked?" He asked.

"Well, I only have a name, and I've talked to the people where he used to work, the drug distributors. I found his name in a directory I got from them. He was young when he worked there. I'm just going down the list of people who were employed at the distributor back in the day, checking them out."

"You think I haven't done that?"

I hesitated for a moment wondering if I had blown enough smoke towards Donahue. I knew that he was bright and probably smart enough to know when he was being yanked around, but I wasn't ready to play all of my cards. When the time is right, I'll call and tell him to look for remains in a hog pen.

"So you haven't really looked for him?"

"I'm pressed for time," I lied. "I thought I'd save a day of running around by checking with the locals before running in circles."

"Do you always let police departments do your dirty work?"

I knew that he knew that I knew more than I was telling him. My gut reaction was to come clean and tell him what I had recorded on my cell phone. Nah..better to keep a few things back. If I was playing poker and had two aces in the hole, I wouldn't bet the limit on the first flop.

"So the answer is yes?"

"I'm not at liberty to answer that question, Yardley. If you know something that I don't, and I find out about it, I'll pound your head in."

"You've already answered my question. Thanks."

I hung up.

From his reaction at the beginning of our conversation, I was pretty sure that the Peoria PD had a missing person file on Cory. One way to find out, find his pretty wife.

CHAPTER 14

Six years had passed since the big drug heist. Things can change in six years. The address that appeared in the distributor's directory for Cory West had not changed. Neither had his pretty wife.

"Yes," she said when she opened the door.

"Mrs. West?"

"I'm Lenore West," she said, hesitatingly, "Who is it you wish to see?"

She was a doll. Long blonde hair hung loosely over her shoulders, her deep blue eyes were staring at me with a troubled question hidden in them. I glanced quickly past her into the living room of the small suburban home. There didn't seem to be anyone else there. I wondered why Cory had gone seeking greener grass with the woman who had repeated his name several times and almost got punched in the mouth for doing so.

"I'm looking for Cory West," I said, although I knew Cory was already pig poop in a God forsaken pen.

"Cory isn't here. Are you from the police? I've told them everything I know."

"When was the last time you saw your husband, Mrs. West?"

That was the best way to avoid her "are you from the police" question. Answer a question with a question. It's an old interviewing technique.

"A week ago today," she said. "Do you have any news about him? Where he might be?"

"No, I'm sorry to say that I do not know his whereabouts, Mrs. West." I lied. A week ago today would be the day I watched her husband eaten by pigs.

"Then how can I help you?"

"Did Cory ever mention a man named Billy Brooks?"

"Cory worked with Billy a long time ago. We haven't seen him in ages. I heard his wife and he have divorced."

"So he hasn't mentioned Billy to you recently?"

"No," she said. "Who are you? Are you from the police?"

"Is your husband in trouble with the police?" I asked. Ask a question in answer to a question, I thought. Old interview technique. Didn't work as well as I'd hoped. Try again.

"If you are from the police you would know." She said, and started to close the door.

I put my foot in the door and said through the small opening.

"I know your husband is missing," I said.

She opened the door slowly.

The deep blue eyes got misty with tears but she held her composure. I've got a weakness for women who cry. It makes me want to hold and comfort them. I wanted to hold and comfort Billy Brooks' wife too. Must be getting soft, I thought.

"Do you know anything about his disappearance?" she asked me.

"He was last seen talking to Billy Brooks," I said. That was the truth, and that was all I was going to tell her.

"Oh. Do you have any idea what he and Billy might have been talking about?"

"I heard the word "suitcase" mentioned," I said. "Did Cory mention a suitcase? Has he traveled recently and had his luggage miss-routed?"

"The last time he went anywhere was almost two months ago," she said. "He went to visit an old college friend in Los Angeles."

"What was the friend's name?"

"Sanders," she said. "Rod Sanders. Cory played football with him in college."

"I thought Cory attended SIU? I know Rod Sanders went to Notre Dame."

"Rod transferred to Notre Dame. Cory stayed at SIU."

"Thanks for clearing that up," I said. "Was it a business trip?"

"I don't think so," she said. "They were just friends. Cory was only gone three days."

"Did Cory receive any mail, phone calls, texts, emails concerning Rod Sanders right before his trip?"

"Not that he mentioned to me," she said. "He was looking through some old papers in his file cabinet one day and I guess he saw Rod's address and phone number. He told me to book him a flight to LA, that he was going to see Rod."

"He didn't call him and announce his plans?"

"He may have when I wasn't around, or when he was out of the house, I don't know."

"What line of work is your husband in, Mrs. West." I was careful to say "is" instead of "was".

"He's an insurance investigator."

"Can you tell me the name of the company?"

"O'Hare Reports," she said. "He's been with them for almost ten years, since he left AngiCal-Garner."

"The pharmaceutical company?"

"Yes. ACG was his first job out of college. He loved that job. I wish he had stayed there, but he insisted that promotions were not going to be imminent and that he could make more money at O'Hare Reports."

"Yes Ma'am" I said, like a bad line from Dragnet.

"Did Cory tell anyone other than you that he was going to visit Rod Sanders?"

"He may have mentioned it in his office," she said. "Cory was rather discreet about most things concerning his work, and it flowed over into our private lives. He didn't talk to me very much about anything, except when he wanted......" She stopped and her blue eyes flickered at me. What she had almost said was clear to me.

"Was Cory in financial difficulties?" I asked. "I don't mean to be personal, Mrs. West, but it is pertinent to our investigation." I acted like I was from the police by using "our" instead of "my".

"No." She said. "I take care of the finances, pay the bills, keep the records and do our income taxes. I would know it if he was having problems with money."

The problems he was having with money were what got him killed, I thought. Maybe not *his* money, but someone's money.

I couldn't think of anything else that I needed to ask, although I was certain that I would think of a dozen things later. She took my silence as a sign that the interview was over.

"If there's nothing else, please remove your foot from my door."

I thanked her and left.

The sun was bearing down on my rental Chevy and the heat inside it was almost unbearable. I turned the air conditioner on full blast and it took a few minutes to get the temperature stabilized at about 75 degrees. Moisture ran down my back as I drove. I had really checked out a lot of clues already in the day and I was already tired. Heat and frustration will make one tired.

I decided to drive back to the motel and relax, get something to eat, then see what Peoria has to offer for entertainment. My swimsuit was an old one and had stretched a little at the waist, but then my waist had stretched a little at the waist also, so I put the swimsuit on, took a large towel from the bathroom and headed for the pool. Minutes later I had swam four lengths of the pool and felt much better. I ordered a Dos Equis from the cute pool-side waitress and asked for a newspaper. Nothing caught my eye in the entertainment section so I flipped to sports and was reading an account of a recent Chicago Bulls and LA Lakers game when a shadow appeared across the page.

I looked up and a man stood three feet from my chaise lounge, looking down at me. The sun was behind him, so his face was featureless.

"Can I talk to you a minute?" The man asked. I recognized the voice. It was the guy who said he was going to shoot me. Here I was with nothing but a newspaper to defend myself, and a half empty bottle of Dos Equis. I felt like I should do something heroic, but couldn't decide what.

"Start talking," I said. "But pull up a chair, the sun's in my eyes."

Ed Stronheim turned away from me and took a chair from a pool-side patio set, I heard it scrape on the concrete as he pulled it closer to me.

"Are you going to shoot me? If so, let me get some clothes on. And shoes. I promised my dear old mother I would die with my boots on."

"I'm unarmed," he said hurriedly. "I just want to talk."

I could see his face after he sat down. He wasn't exactly a lady's man, long face, narrow nose and chin, receding hairline.

"Ah. Well, talking is better than shooting, any old day," I said. "Talk to me."

"I know you talked to my wife."

I tensed. Defense tactic habits are hard to break. With a quick motion, I had my legs off of the chaise lounge, and stood, ready for whatever Ed Stronheim had in mind.

The motion must have scared him. Maybe he thought I was going to kick his head again, he jerked his body back, almost tipping the chair over.

"You're not going to kick me again, are you?"

"Relax," I said. "Sorry if I scared you. It's just habit."

He leaned forward again.

"What I want to talk to you about is Billy," he said.

"I'm listening," I said. I tried not to sound too excited about that development.

"I knew him at Joliet," he said. "He was in the cell next to mine. We talked a lot. He told me about knowing where there was a lot of money. He was ahead of me on the release date but he told me to come and see him when I got out, and we would find the money and split it."

Now I really was interested.

"How much money is a lot of money?" I asked.

"Don't know. Billy never mentioned an amount. He just said he knew where it was and that he could get to it."

"If he knew where it was, why was he always so broke and hard up?" I asked.

"He said he would have to do something for somebody to get his hands on the money."

"Do something *for* somebody or do something *to* somebody?"

Stronheim sat silent for a minute. His face went blank and he stared at me.

"I'm pretty sure he said do something for somebody, but it might have been the other."

"Did he say who the somebody was, or what he had to do?"

"No, he was pretty tight lipped about all of that."

"Why did he want to cut you in?"

"He was pretty sure that it would take two people to do whatever it was that needed to be done."

"Done for somebody or to somebody," I said. "That's the question."

"Anyway, that was before I got out. When I got out I didn't have a job, no place to go and no money. I went to see Billy but he wasn't at the address he gave me. I met his wife. She lived at the address but said that Billy was gone and she didn't know where he was."

"A farm house, south of Peoria?" I asked.

"How'd you know?" He asked me. I shook my head.

"I can't tell you that," I said. "If I did, I'd have to kill you."

His head and shoulders snapped back again, just like they had when I stood up.

"It's just a joke," I said. "Relax. I'm not going to kill anybody today."

"Cindy told me you were a cop. I've been trying my damndest to stay clean. I swear I haven't even talked to Billy. That would be breaking my parole terms. You're not going to report this to my parole officer, are you?"

"Cindy was partially right," I said. "I'm working a case that involves Billy, but I can't tell you much about it. I won't say anything to your parole officer if you tell me what I want to know."

"What is it you want to know?" He asked. "I might not know what you want to hear."

"Did Billy ever mention any names? Did he talk about why he was in prison?"

"He said he took some trailers to Alabama and sold them. That's about all he said. He never mentioned any names in regards to the money."

"OK," I said. "I'll mention some names. You tell me if you've ever heard them before, either from Billy or Cindy."

I started with the name Rod Sanders. He shook his head. I went down the list of names I had in my memory banks that were connected to AGC pharmaceuticals. When I said Marion Ford, an almost imperceptible raising of his eyebrows told me that Ed Stronheim had heard that name. He shook his head negative though. I put that one in a drawer in my old gray matter cabinet and slammed it shut. He knew Marion Ford but for his own reasons didn't want me to know that he knew him.

I didn't pause in my questioning. No need to let him realize that I knew he was holding out on me.

When I finished rattling off every name I could remember, I sat down, picked up my beer and took a long drink. His eyes watched me.

"Can I buy you a beer?" I said.

"No, thanks," he said, looking away quickly.

"So you haven't seen or heard from Billy since you got out? He didn't come around after you and

112

Cindy got hitched, threatening or trying to coerce you?"

"Nope."

"Why do you think he's avoiding you, Ed? After all that talk in prison about knowing where there was a lot of money, why the cold shoulder now?"

"The only reason I can think of is that he doesn't need my help any longer, either to do something *for* someone or *to* someone." He let himself relax enough to grin slightly, then straightened his face again.

"So if he doesn't need you, did he find someone else to help him?"

"I don't know," Ed said, a quizzical look on his face.

"Let me ask you something, Ed." I said, my voice taking on a serious note. "Why did you look me up, find out where I was staying, and come to tell me about Billy and the money? Did someone ask you to tell me? Are you being paid to tell me this? How did you find me here? You must have had some help."

"No help. I've been tagging you since you kicked the shit out of me this morning," he said. "That's how I knew you had talked to Cindy. You're a busy man, Mr. Yardley. I figured it was better to talk to you here in public, than to try to approach you somewhere else and get the shit kicked out of me again."

I didn't exactly swallow that. In the back of my mind I had the notion that Ed Stronheim wasn't afraid of me any more than I was afraid of him.

CHAPTER 15

I slept in the next morning. Not because I was physically tired, but because I didn't have to get up early. I wanted to make the trip to the DMV and I knew they didn't open until 10 so I just stayed in bed, slept awhile, watched a little of the early morning news.

Cory West made the news.

"35 year old Cory West, an insurance investigator from Peoria, has not been seen in a week. His wife reported him missing after he didn't come home for three days. It isn't unusual for him to be gone three days, according to his wife, but when he didn't call or show up on the fourth day, she called the police. If you have seen this man, call 9-1-1 and talk to local missing persons investigators."

They showed a picture of Cory. No mistake about who they were looking for, but no mention that Cory had once worked for AGC distributors at the time of the biggest heist in Illinois history.

Something clicked in the old wheel house of my brain. The truck that Cory and Billy arrived in the day Cory was fed to the pigs should have showed up somewhere. Whose truck was it, Cory's or Billy's? I figured it had to belong to Cory. Billy didn't register in my mind as one who could afford a new truck.

I got my cell phone and replayed the video. The truck was a Dodge Ram 1500. The rear license plate number was plainly visible in the video. Why hadn't I thought of that before? Getting old, Yardley. I played the video again and stopped it when the truck spun around, Billy driving, and left the front yard of the farm house. I grabbed my notebook and a pencil and jotted down the license plate number. It would be easy enough to find out whether Cory or Billy owned the truck, I'd check that when I checked the number on the old car, a 1992 Oldsmobile, that had sat on concrete blocks in the yard the day a satellite snapped pictures.

Breakfast was good in the diner at the motel. I had sourdough toast, eggs and bacon and hash brown potatoes and coffee. Nothing like a good breakfast to start a day.

It looked like rain when I left the motel, dark clouds were rolling in from the west. I was hoping I could get inside the DMV office before the downpour started, but no such luck. I ran from the car to the building, through puddles that appeared suddenly in the asphalt parking lot. Inside there were lines everywhere. Without any idea where to start, I got in the shortest line I could find and waited. Then I waited some more. And I waited another little bit. The line shuffled forward in spurts. Sometimes I would move up two or three spots, other times only one.

I finally got to the DMV clerk. He looked up at me over his bifocals.

"May I have your old license, please."

"Oh, I'm not here to renew my license," I said. "I'd like to know the owners and addresses for two vehicles. I have the Illinois license plate numbers."

"This is the license renewal line," he said. "You'll have to go to the administrator's office to get that information."

"And where would that be?" I asked.

"Around on the other side of the building. Go out the front door, turn left and walk around about half way. You'll see a sign that says "Admin".

"But it's pouring down rain out there," I said. "Isn't there a way to get there from inside?"

"The Administrator keeps that door locked, Sir. You'll have to go around."

No need to argue with city hall. I went back out the front door and waited under an overhang for a minute or two, hoping the rain would let up. It didn't.

I half ran, half walked around the way I was told, not wanting to slip on wet concrete. By the time I reached the Admin office I was pretty much soaked to the skin.

I grabbed the door knob and yanked. It didn't budge. I tried twisting the knob and found that the door was locked.

Retracing my steps, I returned to the main entrance. I went inside and walked an aisle around the interior to the rear of the building. There was another door there with "Admin" on it. I tried the knob and it opened.

I walked in. The office was typical, steel desks, six foot high partitions. In the rear of the office was a room with a door opened to the interior. A cute secretary or clerk of some kind glanced at me and smiled.

"Can I help you, Sir?"

"Have you got a complete set of men's clothes? Size 34 by 32 pants, large tee shirt, size 34 underwear, boxers, not briefs. I need to get out of these clothes before I drown."

She looked at me with a puzzled look.

"Pardon me?"

"Never mind," I said. "The guy where you renew your license said I had to go outside and around to the Admin office. He said the Administrator keeps the inside door locked. I found the opposite to be true."

"Oh," she said, and smiled broadly. "That's when it's not raining. When it rains we lock the outside door. We don't think anyone would be coming in that way."

"I see," I said, although I didn't.

"Can I help you?"

"I have two vehicle license numbers that I would like to check to see who the owners of these vehicles are, and perhaps get their addresses."

"Do you own the vehicles?" She asked. I swear to God, that's what she asked me.

"If I owned them, wouldn't I know who owns them?"

"Oh, yeah. What I mean is, are you from the bank? The bank might own the vehicles, and they may be registered to the person who is buying them."

"Right," I said, sighing. "No, I don't own them. I'm not from the bank."

It was time to show my badge. I pulled out my wallet, flipped it open to the California Private Investigator's badge and flashed it.

"I'm from stolen vehicle section," I said.

"OK." She said. "I can help you. Please tell me the numbers of the plates."

I rattled off the first number and started on the second.

"Wait, one at a time, please," she said. "The computer will not do two at a time."

I waited.

"Can you repeat that number, Sir?"

I repeated it.

The keys on her computer clicked as her long nails clacked across the keyboard. She waited.

I waited.

What seemed like two hours and fifteen minutes later, although it was probably only a half an hour, she turned to me.

"Would you like a printout?"

"That would be nice," I said.

She punched a button on the keyboard and almost immediately a printer in the corner of the room chattered. She got up from her desk, walked to the printer and tore off the sheet, returned to the counter and handed it to me.

"There you go," she said.

"What about the second one?" I said.

"I'll have to put that number in the computer too," she told me. "It won't take two numbers at once."

"Yeah, you mentioned that," I said.

"You can give me the second number now."

I gave it to her.

She typed it in, hit the print button and the printer clacked again. She uncrossed her pretty legs, walked to the corner, tore off the sheet and returned to the counter and smiled.

"See? That wasn't so bad, was it?"

I thanked her, bit my lip hard, and left.

Albert Einstein once said, "Only two things are infinite, the universe and human stupidity, and I'm not sure about the former." The older I get, the less I can tolerate dumb people. I thought about that for a minute then realized that maybe the clerk wasn't so dumb after all. Maybe she intentionally printed the results of the number search one at a time to tease me, mentally. Or physically when she uncrossed her long legs. Maybe the dumb one is me.

By the time I reached the door at the front of the building, the rain had subsided to just a drizzle. I walked quickly back to the car and got in before the skies changed their minds and the rain gushed down some more. The natural light was very poor inside the car so I turned on the roof light and looked at the printouts.

The Dodge Ram was owned by Mr. and Mrs. Cory West. That wasn't a surprise.

The old Monte Carlo was owned by Clifford Stevenson. The man who owned the pig farm.

I started to think about something. Rod Sanders had told me that he owned the house where Billy and Cindy Brooks lived, next to the pen where the hogs lived. Cindy Brooks had told me that Billy worked for the pig farmer. The contract that I had signed with Rod Sanders indicated that the tenants of the house would permit me to enter, and that he was the landlord. Now I was beginning to doubt the veracity of the entire farm house deal. Maybe I had been set up. But if that was true, why? And by whom? I didn't even know Rod Sanders prior to being hired to serve as his security agent for his party. So who would want me to go to a house where there was a chance I might be arrested for breaking and entering, burglary, or even worse, feeding an insurance agent to the hogs?

"Take it easy, old feller," I told myself. "One step at a time, you'll get through this."

Maybe it was time to talk to Clifford Stevenson, to see if he could shed some light on the mysterious house in the corn, and a ruthless killer named Billy Brooks.

CHAPTER 16

It wasn't hard to find the Stevenson house. The address from the old car registration was one that looked familiar to me for some reason, and when I keyed it into the GPS system in the rented Chevy, it popped up near a State Route that was very close to the place where I had searched for the missing suitcase. I remembered seeing the name of a "lane" as I drove down the corn-lined road to the spot with the rubbish and old bicycle in the yard. I remembered it because it had made me think of a time in my childhood. Mulberry Lane. My mind drifted back, as I drove down the blacktopped road, to my earliest memories. My dad had sharecropped a farm less than 300 miles from here, near the Ohio River.

There on that farm was a huge Mulberry tree. My older sisters would spread old sheets under the tree and me and two older brothers would climb the tree and shake the limbs when the mulberries were ripe. The berries would be gathered and made into jelly or pies. Along the front road of that place was an old barbed wire fence where honeysuckles had grown over, the sweet smell of honeysuckles blooming still lingers in the pleasant corners of my memory.

Unlike the former home of Billy Brooks, the house that Stevenson owned was very neat and well kept. A large two story house, long front porch shaded by two giant Mulberry trees. The lawn was freshly mowed and I could smell the grass as I parked the Chevy to the side of a gravel parking area, got out and walked towards the porch.

Before I could climb the stairs and knock on the door, a man appeared on the porch. He wore bib overalls, a blue chambray shirt under the overalls. A gray fedora style hat sat on the back of his head, sweat stain across the front.

"Howdy," he said and raised his right hand to his chest, palm out.

I waved back and smiled.

"Good afternoon, Sir."

He sat down on a porch swing, hauled out a pipe and filled it from a leather pouch that he dug out of the pockets of the bib.

"Might bit warm ain't it?"

"Yes it is," I said, and climbed the steps to the porch.

"I'm Cliff Stevenson," he said.

I walked to the swing and stuck out my hand. He took it with a strong grip and looked up through a haze of smoke that triggered memories of my dad smoking a pipe.

"My names is Kip Yardley, Sir," I said. "I've come all the way from California to do some work. I'm an investigator for a private firm, working on a case that involves the pharmaceutical heist that took place here a few years back."

"Oh yeah," he said. "I remember when that happened. They ain't caught them thieves yet?"

"No, Sir." I said. "There's a Peoria police officer that is dead set on doing that, though."

"Is that right?"

"Yes, Sir. Can I ask you some questions?"

"Well, I don't know nothing about that case," he said. "I just farm and raise hogs. Don't pay much attention to police work."

"Yes, Sir." I said. "What I want to ask is about the house and barn a mile or so from here. An empty house, looks like nobody's lived there for a while. Do you know the one?"

"Why yes, I do know that one. I had some special boar hogs over there for a while, feller by the name of Brooks worked for me. At least he was supposed to work for me. I found out he wasn't doing much work so I fired him, asked him to leave."

"So the house belongs to you?"

"Yep," he said.

"That's funny," I said with a look that must have been quizzical to him.

"What's funny 'bout me owning that house?" He blew a puff of smoke towards me and his voice changed a little, not as friendly as it sounded earlier.

"Nothing is funny about that," I said hastily. "I didn't mean that you owning it was funny, it's just that I was told somebody else owned that place."

"Nope. I've owned it for nigh on to fifty years," he said. "Inherited that old house when my daddy died. I moved momma in with me and she died two years later. I've thought about selling it, but then it ain't worth much and if I ever find someone to tend those hogs, I'll need a place for 'em to stay."

"Yes, Sir."

"What else you want to know, friend? I've got a sandwich waiting for me and I've got a lot of work to do yet. Can't make a living sittin' here smokin' and talkin'."

"How well did you know Billy Brooks?" I asked. He looked at me with a puzzled look.

"Pretty well," he said. "I knew he'd been in the pen, if that's what you're getting at. I figured I'd help him out a bit by giving him a job. He worked OK at first then he got to running around, drinking and gambling. I went over there one day to check on my hogs and found they was mighty poorly looking. He hadn't been feeding and taking care of them. I fired him."

"Did you find someone else to take care of them?" I asked.

"Nope. I've had to go over there nearly every day and haul feed to them on the truck. They have to eat or they'll get a little wild."

"Yes, Sir." I said, thinking of how wild they had gotten.

"When's the last time you were there?" I asked.

"Yesterday," he said.

I felt bad about ripping up drywall in the attic of the house that this old man had probably lived in as a youth.

"I've got a confession to make," I said.

"You ain't run over one of my hogs have you?" he said.

"No. I was hired by a man in California to look in that house, the one next to the pig pen and barn. I was told I'd find a suitcase in the attic behind two sections of drywall. I took a saws-all and cut away parts of that drywall but didn't find a thing. I'll pay you for the damage I caused."

"A suitcase?"

"Yes. It is a leather suitcase, brown, Samsonite." I described the suitcase.

"Might have belonged to Billy Brooks," he said. "Tweren't mine."

"Have you ever seen anyone around that house with a suitcase that matches that description?"

"Can't say that I have," he said.

I stood there for twenty seconds, trying to think if I had covered everything that I wanted to find out by talking to Cliff Stevenson.

"Well, if you want to talk more, come on in and have a sandwich with me," he said, getting up out of the swing. "I gotta get back to work. Will you have a bite to eat?"

"No thank you, Sir." I said. "Here's my card. If you think of anything about Billy that you figure is peculiar or that might relate to the pharmaceutical company's loss, call this number and leave me a message. And send me a bill for the drywall repair, and I'll have my firm send you a check."

He pulled out a dilapidated old wallet, dug through it and handed me a card. It said simply, "C. Stevenson, Farmer" with his phone number.

"Nope. That place ain't worth the postage. I'll call you if I think of something though. Sure you don't want a bite to eat?"

"I'm pretty busy, too, Sir," I said. "Thank you, but no. And thanks for your time."

"Time's free," he said. "But don't waste it. When you get my age you ain't got much left."

We shook hands and I heard the screen door slam as I walked back to my car.

It was getting late and I was getting tired. The trip to the DMV had left me feeling a bit chilled and now I was starting to slow down a little. I glanced at the clock on the dashboard and saw that it was nearly 4. Back on the interstate, I headed towards the airport and my motel.

CHAPTER 17

I opened the door to my room and almost immediately knew that I was in trouble. It was the smell of cigarette smoke. I always ask for a "no smoking" room wherever I travel, and this trip was no exception. But there was the faint, distinct smell of cigarettes in the air when I opened the door.

I glanced around quickly, saw no-one. The reason I didn't see him was because he had been behind the door and whatever he hit me with made a black fog encompass my vision. It was like seeing something one second and nothing the next.

When I came to a conscious state again I could see the bottom of the bed which meant that my head was on the level of the floor. I saw a pair of Wolverine work boots that were definitely not mine, since I haven't worn work boots in 30 years. My eyeballs rolled a little until I could see a pair of white socks and then blue jeans with an inch of the bottom part of each leg rolled up.

I guess I might have moaned a little. I heard a man's voice, high and squeaky, and knew that I recognized it from somewhere. Where had I heard that voice? My mind raced back over the past weeks, like running a cassette tape in reverse, then fast forwarding it until it stops briefly.

"Don't shoot me," I heard the voice say. I could smell a distinct odor, it was pig manure. My brain was playing tricks on me. What just happened and where the hell am I?

Then the voice sounded a little clearer, closer, like someone was speaking directly into my head, bypassing the aural canals, ear drum, sensory nerves.

"Where's the suitcase?"

"What?" I asked. "What just happened? Who are you?"

"I think you know who I am," the voice said. "I think you know a lot more about me than I know about you. Unfortunately that makes you a danger to me and my friends."

I rolled over on my stomach, drew my knees up under me, put the palms of my hands on the floor at shoulder level, and tried to push myself up. Nothing worked. Some part of my anatomy was refusing to obey the commands from my brain.

I was staring at my hands. My wrists were bound together with something that looked like wire from a coffee pot. That's because it was wire from a coffee pot. It finally dawned on me that I couldn't push up because my wrists were tied to the rail of the bed that some idiot sat on, asking me stupid questions about a suitcase.

"So who do you think that I think you are?" I asked, even though the question was a little mixed up and didn't make sense to me. I hoped that it made sense to whomever it was I was speaking to, because it was befuddling as hell to me.

I saw the Wolverine boots move. As one swung past my nose I smelled pig manure again, and when the wearer of the boots lifted his foot I saw dried substance on the bottom that might just be pig manure. The legs encased in blue denims moved past and out of my line of vision. I heard water running in the bathroom, the sound like putting water in a pitcher.

Then I felt the water splashing on my face.

I shook my head.

"You are Kip Yardley, a private dick from L.A. You know who I am because you filmed me throwing a man into a pig pen. I've seen the video on your cell phone. Since you witnessed that event, you life isn't worth a quarter. But before I get rid of you, I want to know where the suitcase is."

I was about ninety eight percent back to full consciousness. I understood who he was, what he was asking, and the imminent dangerous position I was in.

"What makes you think I know?"

"I went back to where I used to live. The drywall had been ripped out, there were footprints on the table, the attic access door had hand prints on it. The video on your cell phone was taken from the attic. I found a saws-all in your car. You're the only one who was looking for the suitcase, and I want it."

"I don't have it." I said. "It wasn't where it was supposed to be. If it's gone, someone beat me to it. *Beat us to it, Billy.*"

I told him about sawing the drywall. I didn't tell him why I was looking for the suitcase in the first place.

"How'd you find me, Billy?" I asked. "Who put you on to me in the first place?"

"You weren't hard to find," he said. "A lady friend of mine told me you were looking for me. So I went looking for you. She said you were from LA so I started checking motels around the airport. She described you. I asked questions. Then when I narrowed it down to this place, I watched for you. I'm not as dumb as you seem to think I am, Yardley."

"No-one said you were dumb, Billy." I said. "You made a bad choice somewhere along the line. What's in the suitcase?"

"What do you think?" he asked. "More money than either of us will ever see in our lifetime. Problem is, it isn't mine. I got paid for a job. The suitcase is a bonus if I can find it, and I think you know where it is."

"Wrong, Billy. I have no idea where it is. If I knew, I'd have taken it back to LA and you and I would never have met under these circumstances."

"Speaking of circumstances," he started, "you've stumbled into something you will not live to regret. Now that you've pretty much convinced me that you don't know the whereabouts of the suitcase, I no longer have a reason to keep you alive. I'm going to take the wires off of the bed-frame so you can get up. I'll also take them off of your ankles so you can walk. Then I've got to dispose of you in a safe place."

"The hog pen?" I said.

"Nah...too risky. Old man Stevenson might show up there. I've got a better idea."

"Forget it, Billy. You're going to dispose of me right here. You think I'm going to get up and walk out of here nice and quiet so you can take me to my final resting place? If you have to kill me, you can do it here. I'm not choosy about where I die."

"I might let you live," he said. "The choice is yours. You leave here with me and you stand a chance on living. If I leave alone, you stay here Dead."

I thought about that for a few seconds. Damned few. He was right and I knew it. If I left with him I was leaving alive and there might be an opportunity somewhere along the way to overpower him. If I didn't leave with him, I'd be left permanently. Discretion, always the better part of valor, won out.

"OK, Billy," I said. "Have it your way.. untie me."

He took the wire from the bed-frame and from around my ankles, all the while holding my gun against the top of my head. I had no illusions about his intent. After all, I'd already seen Billy's ruthlessness. Anyone who would feed a man to the hogs would not hesitate to blow a big hole in my old noggin.

"Get up." He ordered. Stay three steps in front of me. We're going to my truck. You'll drive. If you get any funny ideas about running or drive the least bit carelessly, you'll wind up with absolutely no chance of living. If you be a good little boy, you might live long enough to try to get out of the mess you've gotten yourself into. Comprende?"

"You got it, Billy." I said, and walked ahead of him, through the door and across the poolside area into the parking lot. He nudged me left when we got to the parking lot.

"You know the truck," he said. "It's the one Cory had."

He handed me the keys. "Let's go back to the farm house. If Stevenson's pick-up is by the barn, we'll drive on by. If not, we're going to stop there for a minute."

"Here's the way I see it," Billy said. "You saw me throw Cory to the hogs. He would have killed me and my killing him was self defense. You filmed all of that on your cell phone, and I've got your cell phone. I want to check in that pig pen to see if there's any of Cory left. If not, the only evidence that he was ever in with the hogs is on your phone. I'll dump the phone in the river, then the only evidence will be you. You find the suitcase and bring it to me and I'll let you live. Ten days. That should be long enough for a smart detective like you to find it. If I get it in ten days, you live. Hell, I'll even give you a couple of grand for your troubles. If I don't get that suitcase in ten days I'll come after you. I can kill you from 250 yards away or 2500 miles away, with a phone call, so don't try to cross me."

"No deal," I said. "I've been offered fifty grand for finding it. If I brought it to you then I know you'd kill me, probably like you killed Cory."

"That was self defense, I told you."

"Self defense?" I asked. "He would have lived if you hadn't thrown him over that fence. He had no defense against those hogs!"

"You see it your way, I'll see it mine," he said. "Drive."

I drove. He kept the gun pressed against my rib cage.

"You are wrong about something else, Billy," I said. "That cell phone isn't the only evidence. I copied that file to my laptop and e-mailed a copy to my office computer. I've also shown it to a California cop, a friend of mine." I was lying, but lies can keep you alive if you can tell them convincingly.

"I didn't see a laptop in your room," he said. "I don't believe it. Nice try, though."

"I left it in LA, Billy."

He was silent while that lie sank in.

"Shut the hell up and just drive," he said.

He sat with his back to the door on the passenger side of the truck, the gun pointed at my head. I ran through every movie I'd ever seen where someone slams on the brakes and jumps out of a moving truck to escape. Nothing I visualized seemed like a good idea, so I just drove.

At the house where Cory died Billy ordered me to pull over next to the fence. I eased the big truck to the fence and stopped. He took a pair of handcuffs that he had probably taken from my briefcase and cuffed one wrist, ran the chain through the steering wheel, then cuffed the other wrist.

"You can blow that horn and I can blow your brains out," he said.

He got out and walked the perimeter of the fence looking into the pen. His eyes searched every inch of the muddy, smelly ground. The pigs ignored him. One of the biggest ones followed him, but on the inside of the fence. The rest were laying on the ground, rolling in mud and pig crap. He reached the far side of the fence where it connected to the barn, then slowly returned, eyes still searching.

When he came back to the truck his hands were shaking. It occurred to me that he realized, maybe for the first time, what he had done.

He opened the passenger door and got in.

I sat waiting for whatever he decided to do with me.

He handed me the key to the cuffs and told me to unlock them. I did so.

"Do you mind if I turn on the radio, Billy?" I asked, and leaned forward and punched the on button on the truck's radio. Country music filled the cab immediately.

"Turn it off," he said. "You'll need to hear where I tell you to drive."

The distraction, although insignificant as it seemed, had to work. When I leaned forward, I moved my left hand with the key to my lap and stuck the key in my pocket. He directed me to drive back towards the interstate. Other than "turn left, turn right, slow down, go straight" and a few other commands, Billy sat silent as I drove. A half hour later we were on a country highway. I could see the structure of a bridge ahead of us and guessed that we were south of Peoria, near the point where the Illinois River flowed southwest towards the Mississippi.

It was starting to get twilight. No other traffic was behind me, and only one car passed going the opposite direction.

Billy ordered me to stop the truck in the middle of the bridge. My left wrist still had the handcuff on it but the right cuff hung dangling in my lap. If I could swing the cuff fast enough I might be able to hit him in the face, but to do that before he squeezed the trigger would be nearly impossible.

"Turn it off," he said. I turned the ignition switch and the engine was silent.

He ordered me to stay, like he was talking to a pet dog. He got out on the passenger side and walked around the back of the truck, all the while pointing the gun through the back window at me. A thought flashed through my brain to start the engine, jerk the transmission into reverse and stomp the accelerator. Not enough time.

Billy took my cell phone from his pocket and threw it into the river.

Then he opened the driver's door and ordered me to get out.

I got out and looked over the railing to the water. It wasn't far, maybe 30 feet to the surface of the dark, fast moving water.

"Snap that other cuff on your wrist," he said.

I snapped it.

"Sit down and put your legs over the edge," he demanded.

I knew what was coming. It was the river or the morgue. Or both. I sat down.

The bridges girders formed a big "X" with a space at the bottom of the "X" just big enough for a man to sit down and fit his head and shoulders under the guard rail. I fully expected that Billy would shoot me in the back of the head and then push me into the river.

He surprised me. He didn't shoot me.

He just pushed me into the river, handcuffed.

CHAPTER 18

The cold, dark water surged over my feet, legs, then chest as I started under. I took a great big lung full of air and before my head went under I was moving my left hand towards the pocket where I had put the key.

Have you ever tried to get your hand into a pocket of wet jeans? With it cuffed to your other hand? I don't know how many seconds it took, I wasn't counting. The only thing I remember is I was struggling hard trying not to suck in water instead of air. My chest was heaving. I finally found the key with my middle and forefinger on my left hand, grasped it as firmly as I could and worked it up inside the wet pocket carefully. When it was near the top I exchanged my thumb for the middle finger, and squeezed the key like there was no tomorrow. If I dropped the damned thing there wouldn't be a tomorrow.

Fortunately I had purchased the cuffs with a slightly longer chain between the two than is standard, sometimes it is difficult to get a big man's arms far enough behind him to cuff him with the short chain between the two cuffs. I'm guessing that the chain was at least 15 inches.

Still holding my mouth tightly shut, and chest heaving, I managed to get the key into the slot. I had my eyes closed at first but opened them long enough to try to find the slot, and realized I couldn't see further than my hands. The water was dark and cold, and swift. I could feel myself being swept downstream, and suddenly it occurred to me that the bridge wasn't more than a half a mile from one of the 8 locks and dams in the river before it empties into the Mississippi. If I was swept into one of them, I could kiss my butt goodbye.

I still had the key in my vise-like grip between thumb and forefinger on my left hand, and turned. Wrong way. I turned it the opposite way and it wouldn't move. I brought my hands near my eyes and saw the problem. The key and chain were encased in a big wad of some kind of water-weed. My mind, fighting a lack of oxygen, remembered fishing in rivers and streams when I was a young kid. I had often pulled up more water-weeds on a hook than I did fish. I brought my hands to my mouth and clinched weeds between my teeth and pulled. Water got in my mouth and it was all I could do to keep from inhaling it. I yanked at the weed and turned the key again. It clicked and strangely I could hear the sound under water. The cuff sprang open and loose from my right hand. I kicked hard and moved my arms down, mustering as much power as I could in oxygen starved muscles.

A split second before I could stand it no longer and inhaled, my head and mouth cleared the surface. Air !!!

I sucked air in huge gasps, spitting water between inhaling. The taste in my mouth was terrible, like a mouthful of mud. My nostrils flared and I smelled the water. It smelled like pig crap. Although it was nearly dark, I could see trees along the bank. I swam with every ounce of strength I had left towards the shore. For every yard I made towards shore, I was swept ten or more downstream.

A quiet roar came to my ears and my alarm went off. The dam! I could hear it, but had no idea how far away it was. Unfortunate for me, water was being released to the next lower level. That meant there would be a powerful suction at the surface, and I realized I didn't have the strength left to keep from being pulled under. I had to make it to the bank before I reached the dam.

Now I was a body length away from bank. The water was still too deep to reach bottom with my legs, so I kept my arms moving in what I thought were powerful strokes, but probably were more like a puppy dog-paddling.

Downstream I glimpsed a tree limb sticking out over the river. I was moving towards it at about ten yards per second. I had just enough time to judge its height above the surface before I swung both arms as high above my head as I could. My right hand missed the branch but the left arm hit it, about half way between wrist and elbow. As the limb scraped under my forearm, I opened my fingers and wrapped them around it, immediately closed them again. The limb wasn't much bigger than a golf club handle.

My body was swept past the tree with such a force that my hand was pulled towards the end of the limb, snapping small twigs that were growing perpendicular to the branch, and ripping the skin on the palm. Pain surged through my hand and up my arm.

I held on. When the limb was swept around the body of the tree by the force of the water, my hand was forced further down the limb, scraping hide from the palm a second time. I felt like screaming. I heard a crack and thought the limb had broke, but it hadn't completely. It just split from the main body slightly. I got my other hand on the branch and worked hand over hand, struggling against the force of the water, until I reached the limb, then wrapped my arms around the limb and held on, resting and clenching my teeth.

Bit by bit I worked my way towards the bank, along the limb. I was kicking with my legs at the same time I was pulling with my arms and hands. Finally I could feel the bottom with my feet. I stopped again, rested, then with what might have been the last effort my tired old arms could possibly make, I got to the main body of the tree, worked my way around it, wrapped my legs and rested some more. I was out of the river.

I pulled myself up the tree trunk, made sure I was on dry ground and wouldn't slip and fall back into the river, then jumped as far as my legs would spring, and landed on hands and knees in grass. I stretched out on the damp grass and lay still, breathing rapidly, and praying once again. I said a prayer to the God I had learned to trust, and thanked him for my life.

`Cold, wet, and worn out, I closed my eyes and let myself relax bit by bit. Slowly I drifted into a shallow sleep. The sleep could not have been more than 5 or 10 minutes but I felt a little better when I woke up. It was completely dark and I was a quarter of a mile from the highway. I could see lights from cars passing, one every 10 minutes or so. I got up and started walking upstream, back towards the bridge and the highway. I hadn't walked more than thirty yards until I had to stop. A ten foot high chain link fence was blocking my way. Across the top of the fence was barbed wire. I realized that it was protective fencing to keep fishermen from trying to fish near the dam. Problem now is how do I get over it?

I turned right and followed the chain link fence another 30 yards, looking for a way to get over it. Instead I found a way to get under it. A ditch ran perpendicular to the fence, then made a right hand turn and ran towards the river. There was a gap between the bottom of the fence and the bottom of the ditch, but there was water in the ditch, probably two feet judging from the width of the ditch. I eased into the water and waded towards the gap. When I reached it, I realized I'd have to duck almost under water, move under the fence, then submerge on the other side. I had no desire to get my head under water again for the next thirty years or so, but I had to get back to the highway. I held my breath and ducked. I moved my head under the fence and scraped the bottom of the chain links on my left ear as I brought my head back to the surface.

But, I was under the fence. Using the fence as a handhold, I pulled myself out of the ditch and once again headed for the highway and the bridge.

CHAPTER 19

I don't know how long it took me to reach the highway. I was exhausted by the time I got there. In the distance I could see the lights of Peoria. I waited for a vehicle to come by so I could try to flag them down. Minutes went by, nothing..then suddenly I heard the sound of a motorcycle and the wavering, up-and down, bounce of a headlight appeared coming fast. Not much chance of getting a ride to town on that, I thought. But something is better than nothing and my odds hadn't exactly been against me the past few hours. I'd survived.

I started waving my arms up and down when the motorcycle was fifty yards away from me. It roared by without slowing, then I saw its brake light come on, go off, and come back on several times. It was slowing. It made a U-turn in the highway and came back slower. It passed me and made another U-turn and stopped a few feet from where I stood.

"What's up?" A deep voice said.

"I fell in the river upstream, and just got out," I said. "I need a ride back to Peoria.

I'll pay you for the trip." I wondered if I still had my wallet, and patted my right front pocket. It was still there. Billy hadn't found it while I was knocked out, another piece of luck.

"You're gonna freeze," the voice said. "I'll give you a ride. You don't have to pay me."

He swung his leg off of the motorcycle and motioned with his right hand for me to get on the buddy seat. I could hardly lift my leg over the bike, but managed to get on. He swung his leg back over and settled his body further up on the seat.

"Man, you don't smell goo good," he said. "Good thing I came along, no one in a car would give you a ride."

With a slight screech of his back tire, he let the clutch out, and off we went. I guessed that we were at least fifteen miles from my motel. Immediately I felt the cold night wind whistle through me. My short sleeve shirt and jeans wasn't keeping any of the wind off of me. I was shivering like a dog pooping peach seeds. It's a wonder I didn't cause the bike to turn over, I was shaking so bad.

I closed my eyes and tried to calm down, meditate. There's a technique I've used often, visualizing a water fountain spraying high into the air and watching the drops fall back into a rippled surface. It has always worked good in the past when

I wanted to meditate, but now I couldn't visualize water. Water was the last thing I wanted to visualize. Instead, I tried concentrating on visualizing a hot tub with bubbling water foaming around me, warm, soothing water.

The water thing had to go.

I tried blanking my mind.

I concentrated on the sound of the motorcycle engine and the wheels on the pavement. I could, after a few minutes, feel a little heat coming from the exhaust pipe. After a few more minutes I felt better, the wind was no longer cold, just cool.

We passed the road that turns off to the old farm house and I knew we would be approaching the exit to the Interstate towards the airport. I leaned forward and spoke as loud as I could. "Take the Interstate north, that's where my motel is."

"OK" I heard roar past my ears.

When we finally arrived at my motel, I pulled my soggy wallet from my jeans and managed to get a twenty out.

"Take this," I said. "You've been a great help."

"Thanks," he said, and took the twenty. "Hey, what about your car? How did you get out there to the river?"

"Long story," I said. "Thanks for the ride."

"No problem."

I still had my wallet in my hand and dug my room card out and headed for my room. I was careful about opening the door, pushed it open, waited a few seconds then went in fast, looking first left, then right. No one was waiting to clobber me. I turned and shut the door and put the latch on, flipped on the light and started peeling off wet clothing. My socks were the hardest to get off. Aching arms just didn't want to reach that far down.

Eventually I was in the shower, letting hot water pour over me. The motel provided a bath soap and I think I used two bars of it scrubbing. I shampooed my hair twice, rinsed it, and just stood there, relaxing. I was so tired I wanted to just sit down and let the hot, soothing water pour over me.

After what seemed like five minutes but was probably closer to fifteen, I felt warm enough and clean enough to turn off the shower, dry myself off and get in the bed. I was asleep in seconds. The last thing that I thought of before conking out was throwing Billy over the fence to a herd of starving wild pigs.

CHAPTER 20

Sunlight streaked between the drapes and the edge of the window and fell across my face. I opened one eye, looked at the clock, then opened the other. It was nearly 10 a.m.

I had slept for almost 12 hours straight.

I used the room phone and called AT&T and made arrangements to pick up another cell phone. Then I called Donahue.

"Where's my beer?" He asked, as soon as I told him my name.

"You'll get it," I said. "First, let me tell you where I've been. I went for an unexpected swim in the Peoria River."

"We've got a swimming pool in town," he said. "Don't they have one at the motel where you're staying?"

"Yeah. The river wasn't my choice, though. I was pushed."

I told him about being conked on the head in my room, the ride to the bridge, and the way I had cheated death by getting out of the river.

"I know the spot," he said. "You're lucky. You were probably no more than a thousand yards from the lock and dam."

"Tell me about it," I said. "Let me give you a name. Billy Brooks. He's the jerk that pushed me in, handcuffed, at that."

"Brooks? The guy that tried to sell trailers and went to the pen?"

"One and the same," I said. "He had something to do with the unsolved case you're working, I'd bet on it."

"We'll put an APB out on him. What kind of car was he driving, or did he take yours?"

"No, mine's still here at the motel. He was driving a new model Dodge Ram 1500, blue. Illinois license plate.....just a minute, I've got that written down."

I found my notebook and gave him the license number.

"The truck is registered to Cory West, Insurance Investigator."

"The missing person's case you asked about!" He said.

"Yep. I think West was on to something about the heist. And I know where he is, that is I know where he was when he died." I told him about the scene I had filmed on my cell phone.

"Bring me that phone, Yardley," he said. "And I told you what I'd do if you held back on me."

"I would have given you that earlier, but I had to check something first. I'll explain later. I can't bring you the phone. Billy threw it in the river. Same bridge he threw me from."

"I'll send a dive team out there and see if they can find it," he said. "Meantime, you'd better come in and give a complete statement, one I can annotate and make part of the case. And the missing person's case. Homicide will want in on it, too."

"Sorry, Donahue. I can't do that. I'll be busy."

"Doing what? You're up to your ass in mud with me now, Yardley. You'd better come in to my office, and bring two cases of Bud-Lite with you."

"I'll be in when I've got something new," I said. "Maybe by then I'll owe you three cases."

I hung up the phone. There was something else I needed to do. I needed to get another gun. My next encounter with Billy Brooks might get a little rough.

A cousin of mine from my home town had been a police officer in a little town in Indiana. He obliged me by meeting me half way at Fairfield, Il and handed me a Taurus 9mm that was the same size as the Ruger 9 that Billy was now carrying. It fit my shoulder holster nicely.

"It's not registered to anyone," he told me. "Indiana's gun laws are not as strict as Illinois, but I hope you don't have to use it. If you say you got it from me, I'll deny it."

"No problem," I told him. "And thanks."

The long drive back to Peoria gave me a lot of time to think about the case. I felt that I was on to something with the connection between Billy and Cory, but I had no idea what the connection might be. If Cory had indeed found evidence of a suitcase stuffed with the proceeds of the heist, in cash, then there should be some record in his file, his computer, or somewhere, that would help me. Should I go digging for that information, or should I hunt down the douche-bag that pushed me, handcuffed, into the river.

As human nature would have it, my desire for revenge answered the question for me, and I had an idea. I knew that Billy liked to gamble, and he liked to drink. The next question was, where? I thought that Cindy Brooks might have information that would help me find him. And so it was, late in the evening, that I pulled the rented car up in front of the apartment where I had talked to Cindy. I didn't particularly want to talk to her new husband, I still didn't trust him much not to shoot me as he promised, but if he was there, I'd question him too.

And as it turned out, Stronheim answered the door when I rang the bell.

"Hello," I said. "I'm not here to see Cindy, particularly, so if you plan on shooting me, think about it."

He grinned. "Come in," he said. "I'm not going to shoot anyone."

I went in.

"Cindy, Hon, we've got company," he called out.

She appeared out of the kitchen area and stopped when she saw me. I thought I saw a faint glimmer of fear cross her face, but it may have been just a shadow.

"Hi again," I said.

"Hello, Mr. Yardley," she said. "This is my husband, Ed." She motioned towards Ed who was still holding the door open.

"We've met." I said, and Ed echoed me.

"I just have a couple of more questions that I'd like to ask, Cindy," I said.

"OK"

"I'm looking for Billy. I understood from our first conversation that Billy likes to gamble and drink. Can you tell me any of the places where he used to hang out?"

"Most of the time he gambles at the Pair-O-Dice hotel riverboat," she said. "That's the main boat, not the hotel. Billy always thought it was cool to gamble and drink on a boat, kind of like Maverick."

"Any other places?"

"Well there were several," she said. Ed stood at the door, listening.

"The main ones," I said.

"When he had won a little, he played at the Pair-O-Dice. When he was low on money, he played at Bust-Em-Up pool hall, near downtown."

"He gambled on pool?"

"Not much," she said. "He wasn't that good of a pool player. The Bust-Em-Up has a basement with card games going. It's illegal, but that's where he played some. He never cared much whether a place was legal or not. He thought that the City people were getting a cut from the licensed places, and always said that was the reason he had better luck at local places."

She gave me the names of three more "illegal" places, the Round Up, the Depot, and Jack's Back.

I wrote them all down in my notebook. I'd start with the Bust-Em-Up first and work my way down the list of "illegal" places before I tackled the Pair-O-Dice.

I thanked her and told Ed I'd see him around. He grinned at me, shook my hand and said, "Good Luck."

I drove downtown and parked in the city lot. I paid my two dollars, got a ticket, and asked the gate-man how to find the Bust-Em-Up.

"Right at the next corner, second place on your right."

I walked the short distance and sauntered in like I knew what I was doing. Actually. I've shot a little pool in my life and knew what I was doing, but there was no way I was going to get snookered into a game of eight-ball in a town where Minnesota Fats had once played Willie Mosconi a three game set of eight ball for ten grand a ball. According to legend, Fats won the break in game one, ran the table and made the eight. It was then Mosconi's break. He ran the table but missed the eight. Fats made six straight but left the 9 ball on the edge of a corner pocket. Mosconi then made the eight. In the third game, Fats ran the table again and made the eight.

I got an RC cola and a bag of peanuts and stood watching a close eight ball game. A young man with spiked hair and a dangling ear ring asked if I wanted to play a game. I agreed and we played. I won with a bank shot of the eight after see-sawing the lead back and forth.

"I like to play for a dollar a ball," spiked-hair said.

"No thanks," I said. I knew a hustler when I saw one. "I really wanted to get in on the poker action. How do I find my way to the games?"

He looked at me, then looked around the room. With a sly look and a motion he ushered me to a door, opened it, and slid aside as I walked in. There was nothing in the room except a large billiards table.

"Push the middle diamond on this side of the table," he said, and stepped out, leaving me alone in the room.

I found the middle diamond, set in ivory, in the red felt side of the table. I pushed it. The table fell slowly away, swung down on springs and hydraulic levers and revealed stairs going to a lighted hall below. I went down the stairs and followed the hall.

At the end there was a door with a knob. It was locked. A small sign in red, was above the knob. I had to bend forward to read it in the dim light.

" Ring for service."

I scanned the door frame, looking for a button but didn't see one. I put my right hand on the top of the frame and felt across it. Near the center was a button. I pushed it and waited.

A few seconds later the door opened. A big man with a shiny bald head and big nose opened the door.

"Five hundred dollar buy in. One, five and ten. Three raises."

I glanced around the room. There were three tables, two of which were full, and six people at the third. I didn't see Billy.

"I was just looking for someone," I said.

"Looking?" he said. "Now if you're through looking, please go back up to the pool hall. This ain't free down here."

"Maybe you know the guy," I said, and described Billy. "His name is Billy Brooks."

"Yeah, I know him." The big man said. "Ain't seen him tonight. Try the Round Up."

"Thanks," I said and left.

Back upstairs I found ear ring boy and got directions to the Round Up. It was a bar in the seedier side of the downtown area, like a lot of cities, there were stores with plywood in place of windows and "for lease" signs abounding. The Round Up had fresh paint on the brick front walls. A lasso rope was painted above and around the door and a new neon light flicked on and off with a blue halo. "Round Up".

Inside, the bar was on the left, a few tables with four chairs at each on the right, and a small dance floor in the rear, then a wall. I surmised that it was behind that wall where poker tables would be found.

I sat at the bar and listened to a half-way decent country band playing. A young male vocalist was singing, "...she's a good hearted woman, loving a good timing man."

Not as good as Waylon, but decent. I watched the dancers moving rhythmically to the beat.

I ordered a bourbon and water and sat sipping it. A woman in her forties slid up on the barstool next to mine and looked at me through false eye-lashes.

"Hi. I'm Lucille."

"You picked a fine time to greet me, Lucille," I said, grinning.

"Funny," she said, but smiled. "Can you buy a lady a drink?"

I looked all around the place slowly, then back at her. "I'm sorry," I said. "I don't see any ladies."

That didn't faze her much either.

"One last chance, Mister," she said. "Most people who come in here need one of three things. Number one, sex. Number two, talk, Number three, drink. Which category do you fall under?"

"I'll take door number two," I said.

"That'll be a brandy and water," she replied. I motioned for the bartender and ordered it for her.

"Do you know Billy Brooks?" I asked.

"Sure. Everybody knows Billy."

"Has he been in tonight?"

"Yep."

"Is he still here?"

"He might be."

"Getting behind door number two is getting tough, Lucille." I said. "Maybe I'll cancel that brandy and water."

"Getting to the brandy and water was tough," she said.

"OK," I said. "You win. Is Billy back there?" I nodded towards the rear wall.

"Yep," she said. "You want me to go get him?"

"Is there a back door?"

"Yes and no. There's a stairway that goes down to the cellar. People that want out real fast will take the stairway, go to the cellar then up a stairs that goes to the back alley, through that door and their gone. Magic. Disappear into the thin pig shit air."

I pulled a twenty from my wallet and put it under her ashtray.

"Give me ten minutes, then go tell Billy a LA Private Eye named Yardley wants to see him out front."

"That's all that is worth?" She smiled, pointing at the twenty. "A brandy and water and your drink will add up to ten. All I get is the change, a measly ten bucks? For another ninety I'll give you more than you've ever had."

I put another twenty down. "At my age, Lucille, I've already had too much. If that isn't enough, forget it," I said. "I'll go get him myself. Of course there may be some rough stuff back there and some of your customers might get disturbed."

"We've been raided a hundred times," she said. "Cops just turn over tables, take the cash and leave. They never arrest anyone.."

"I'm not a cop," I said. "What I meant by rough stuff is bullets flying."

Her eyes got a little bigger behind the false eye-lashes, and the ton of make-up failed to cover the sudden pallor in her cheeks. I pulled back my jacket and showed her the nine.

She picked up the two twenties and moved away.

"Ten minutes," I reminded her.

She turned back towards me, winked and gave me a thumbs up.

I drained my bourbon and water, sat the glass down and walked outside. The Round Up was in the middle of the block and I mentally flipped a coin as to which way I should go, turned left and walked rapidly to the corner, made a left and then another left down a dark alley. Only then did it occur to me that I didn't know which door in the alley would be the one Billy would come through when he left the Round Up's cellar.

I stopped and focused my mind on the street front. There had been a boarded up place, then an antique shop, then a typewriter repair shop (although there probably hadn't been a typewriter repaired in it for forty years), and then a pawn shop on the corner. I thought carefully about it. Yes, that was what I had seen after leaving the Round Up.

I counted to the fourth door as I walked down the alley, found the hinges on it in the dim light, and stood to the left of the hinges and waited.

It didn't take the full ten minutes for me to get in place and Lucille hadn't given me the full ten minutes. Whether she wanted to let Billy get away or whether she just plain didn't like me, I don't know. But in my mental clock only about seven minutes had passed. Suddenly I heard the sound of heavy footsteps running up the stairs from the cellar below. A scraping sound screeched as a bolt was thrown on the door, then the door swung open, dim light escaping into the dark alley.

Billy Brooks bolted from the open doorway, moving fast. I was prepared, and moved a little bit faster.

I swung the 9MM hard at the base of Billy's head, not hard enough to knock him out, but plenty hard enough to knock him down.

He landed on hands and knees, slumped to his chest, his hind end still up in the air, then slowly collapsed, face down.

He moaned a little but I was sure he wasn't out.

"Get up, Billy," I said. "We're going for a little ride."

I pulled his arms up behind him and cuffed him. It might be time for Billy to go for a swim in the murky waters of the Illinois River.

CHAPTER 21

I could not hold Billy's weight out over the water, like I wanted to do, so I made him sit in the same spot I had sat, and put my foot between his shoulder blades.

"Now, Billy, tell me about the heist at the place you used to work."

"I don't know anything about that heist," he said.

I pushed a little with my foot.

"What's in the suitcase, Billy?"

"Money. I told you that. More money than you and I will ever see unless we find it."

"We?"

"I'm offering you a deal, Yardley. Help me find that suitcase and I'll give you half of it."

"No deal," I said. "If I find it, I'll return it to LA and collect my fifty grand, then I'll turn this whole bad nightmare over to the police."

"If you know what's good for you, you'll help me," he said. "People are already starting to talk about you. You're getting to be pretty well known."

"What people, Billy?"

"Oh, you know, the ones that might have a stake in finding that suitcase."

"So you don't know anything about the heist, but you know there 's money in that suitcase?"

"What heist?"

I pushed a little harder on his back.

"One last chance, Billy." I said. "Who organized the heist?"

"Get it over with, Yardley," he said. "If you push me in the river, I'm gone. If I tell you what I know and my friends find out I told you, I'm gone anyway. Six of one, a dozen of the other."

I wasn't quite sure I knew how he did his math, but that's what the man said.

He was being a lot tougher to crack than I expected him to be, and I wasn't sure what I should do next. If I pushed him a little harder he was going to drown. I'd be responsible for killing him, just like he was responsible for killing Cory. I'm not a killer, although I've dispatched a few bad guys that were trying to dispatch me.

I thought about it for a minute or so, changed my entire game plan, and pulled Billy back away from the river's edge. My bluff hadn't worked and there was no need to continue along that line.

"Come on, Billy," I said. "I've got someone who wants to meet you."

I got him back in the car and undid the cuffs on his left hand, passed the chain through the armrest on the passenger side, and cuffed his hand again. That's the way I'd transported him to the bridge.

"Remember, Billy, this gun I've got pointed at you is not registered. I won't hesitate to bloody up this car a little if you try anything funny."

He sat silent while I drove.

My idea had been to scare the crap out of him and see if he would open up about who had helped pull off the biggest heist in Peoria's history. My idea failed. Now I had no idea and was beginning to think that the entire trip to the bridge was wasted time.

I used the cell phone that AT&T had given me to call Donahue.

"Donahue," he answered.

"I've got Billy," I said.

"I figured it was you," Donahue said. "I just left The Roundup and Lucille told me there was a dude who'd asked for Billy."

"Are you at your office?" I asked.

"On the way there. Bring him to me."

"OK." I said. "I'll be there in a half an hour."

Billy was silent as I drove.

"You're a funny guy, Billy," I said. "You're a lot tougher inside than I figured you to be. You're smarter than I gave you credit for being, but you've screwed up big time now. You'll be charged with Cory's murder, somehow or another, I'll tie you to the heist, and I'd expect you'll get at least twenty years for that offense. So what's it going to be? Do you feel like talking now?"

"You should have pushed me in the river, Yardley," he said.

"I couldn't do it. I'm not as cold blooded as you are. But when they strap you down and stick that needle in your arm I'll be there to witness it."

"Screw you, Yardley."

I knew when I was beat. Billy was more afraid of the people he was in cahoots with than he was of anything I could threaten him with. He'd shown that fear at the river and was now affirming it. It was out of my hands. I'd played my top cards with Billy, now it was up to the State of Illinois to see what they could do.

On the way in to Peoria proper I stopped at a liquor store and bought two cases of Bud Lite and a case of Dos Eqis.

Donahue's door was open and I ushered Billy in ahead of me.

"Billy, this is Donahue," I said.

Donahue stood up and walked around his desk and put his own handcuffs on Billy's wrists.

"Take yours off," he told me. I complied.

"Sit down, Billy," he said, shoving Billy backwards towards a chair. Billy sat down hard and his head bounced off of the wall behind him. I wasn't sure I wanted to see any more, but Donahue shut the door and motioned for me to have a seat.

"We can make this easy or we can make if difficult," Donahue said.

"We can make it with an attorney present," Billy said.

"OK," Donahue said. "You have a right to keep silent......" He recited the Miranda clause.

"I'm going to ask a few questions, Billy," Donahue said after he had advised Billy of his rights.

"I'm taking the fifth," Billy said, grinning.

Donahue got up from his desk, walked around it, and slapped Billy across the face with an open handed slap that rocked Billy's head.

"You sonofabitch!" Billy said.

Donahue swung open handed with his left hand and rocked Billy's head back the other way.

"Did you see that big mosquito on Billy's face, Yardley? I tried to keep it from biting old Billy, but it just flew to his other cheek."

Billy sat staring at Donahue.

"You wouldn't be so damncd frcc with your hands if mine weren't cuffcd," Billy said.

"Stand up, Billy," Donahue said.

Billy remained seated.

Donahue grabbed a fistful of Billy's shirt with one hand and raised Billy out of the seat, shoved him to the wall and let go. Billy stood there glaring at Donahue.

Donahue took the cuffs off of Billy and turned his back on him completely, dropping the cuffs on his desk. I sensed what was coming. Billy drew back his right arm and swung at the back of Donahue's head. Donahue moved slightly and rapidly to his right so Billy's punch missed. Donahue grabbed Billy by the back of the neck and slammed his head down on the edge of the desk. I heard the "chunk" and saw red splatter across the front of the desk.

"Had enough, Billy?" Donahue said, still holding him by his neck.

"Oomph."

Donahue jerked back with his left hand, snapping Billy's head. I thought he was going to slam Billy's head on the desk again, instead he shook Billy like a rat terrier would shake a rat. When he let go of Billy's neck, Billy staggered backwards, the back of his knees hit the edge of his chair and he sat down hard.

"OK," Donahue said. "Let's try this again. I'm going to ask some questions, Billy. You can refuse to answer them. There are a whole lot of mosquitoes flying around in here though, aren't there, Mr. Yardley?"

I kept quiet.

"Who you working for, Billy?"

Silence.

"What was Cory's part in this, Billy? By the way, we know about Cory and the pigs."

Silence.

Donahue was standing in front of the seated Billy. When he drew back his hand to slap Billy the third time, I spoke up.

"Hold it," I said.

Donahue looked at me.

"He won't talk." I told him about threatening to push Billy handcuffed into the river.

"You should have pushed the little prick," Donahue said. "That would have saved the State of Illinois the expense of trying him."

"I know what it's like to be swept downstream in the river, handcuffed," I said. "I couldn't do it. I'm not as ruthless as Billy."

I could see the relief in Billy's face. He wasn't going to talk, the resolve was evident, but so was the relief.

Donahue cuffed Billy's hands behind him this time and then motioned toward the door. "Let's book him," he said.

CHAPTER 22

It didn't take me long to find out where Billy had been staying. The room was above an old baseball cap factory on the edge of town where things were so rough the Mafia wore bullet proof vests. The old dame that showed me where the room was could have been nice looking at one time or another, but age, liquor and probably disease had left her looking like the wicked witch of the west. I told her I was a cop and she didn't even ask for proof, she just waddled down the hall and I heard her footsteps descending back to her place on the first floor.

The door was locked. Back in LA I had a ring of keys that would open almost any locked door. Now I had nothing but my pocket knife and my feet. I kicked the door open with my right foot and slammed my back to the wall on the right of the door outside the room. No gunshots rang out and

I could see a portion of the interior of the room. It looked safe enough. I went in.

There was a cot like bed, a small four drawer chest with a hot plate and a coffee pot on it. To my left was a door that was open. I could see part of a toilet seat and a tub with a dirty shower curtain hanging inside of it.

I started with the bed. There was nothing there that caught my eye. The four drawer chest had an assortment of tee shirts, socks and underwear but nothing else. A closet with no door on it revealed a few pairs of pants and one seedy looking sports coat. I searched through the pockets. Nothing. The bathroom was pretty dirty but I found nothing there. A razor, a can of Burma Shave and a toothbrush and almost empty tube of toothpaste was all there was in the medicine cabinet. I took it off of the wall and looked behind it and in the space between the wall. Nothing.

I sat on the edge of the bed and looked around the room. Where would I hide something if I was living in this dive, on the edge of eternity, waiting for something to happen that would make me extremely wealthy? What was it that Billy knew about the heist or about the suitcase? Why did Cory think that Billy knew where the suitcase was hidden? If Billy knew the location of the suitcase, and it was full of cash like he said it was, he would have been long gone. Probably in Las Vegas, gambling and living the fast life.

Nope. Billy knew nothing about the location of the suitcase. He might have known at some point, but either he had been double crossed, double crossed someone or had found the suitcase or was totally innocent of the heist. I didn't like the second scenario but the first one had possibilities. Why had Sanders pointed me to the farmhouse attic? Had the suitcase ever been there? Billy had said something about it NOT being where he put it, but he didn't say he had put it in the farmhouse.

I hadn't expected to walk in to Billy's abode and find directions to the suitcase. I really didn't know what I was looking for, but the guess, dancing around in my head, was a letter, a document of some kind, or a name that might lead me to the people Billy was protecting. There was a Peoria telephone book on the table, it appeared to be one of the last ones published by Yellow Pages with household numbers. I picked it up and thumbed through it looking for numbers that might be marked, underlined or circled. I shook it. A newspaper clipping fell out. It was a public notice that all items in the city impound lot would be auctioned at the lot on Sunday, August 15th. It didn't seem important to me but for some reason, but I stuck it in my shirt pocket.

Other than that, I found nothing. Nothing, that is, except Billy's parole papers. Even if my old cell phone, with the incriminating evidence to get Billy convicted of murder, was never found, he could be held for violating his parole. Parole violation was a walk in the park compared to feeding a man to the pigs.

I stuck the parole papers in my jeans pocket and left the room more or less the way I'd found it, with the exception of the broken latch on the door.

I drove back to my motel room and sat in the chair watching the Lakers play basketball until I got sleepy, turned off the TV and went to bed. Tomorrow's another day, I thought. If I don't find another clue soon, I'll be catching a flight back to LA and to hell with the suitcase.

CHAPTER 23

Tomorrow was another day. That is today is another day. I'm sitting in my room at the motel, pondering what clues I had left, what the situation was with the case, and trying to decide whether to fold or ante when the phone rang. I nearly jumped out of my hide. I'd not expected anyone to call me, had even forgotten who I had given my motel number to, let alone who might be calling me.

It was Richard Rheames.

"As I live and breathe," I said. "I was just thinking about you."

"Not hardly, Kip Yardley," Richard said, in his rhyming jingle retort. "You probably haven't thought of me since you called me last."

"Well, to be truthful, I've ran out of clues, and I'm glad you called. What did you find on that scrap of aluminum I sent you?"

"A number."

"A full number?"

"No, a fraction," he said, sarcastically, "Of course it's a full number, anything over a fraction of a number is a full number isn't it?"

I didn't reply because I wasn't sure of the logic of that statement.

"Give it to me," I said, picking up a pen and pulling the motel stationary pad closer.

"It's a phone number, by the looks of it," he said. "Are you ready, Teddy?"

"Fire, when ready, Freddy," I said.

He laughed.

"Area code, 812," he said, and gave me the rest of the number. I wrote it down.

"Where's area code 812?" I asked.

"Next door to Illinois, boy," he said.

"North, South, East, or West?"

"East. It's Indiana."

"Good work, Richard," I said. "Thanks. I owe you one."

"That's going to cost you more than one," he said. "Two Dodger games and a lunch at Der Weiner Schnitzel."

I figured that the hot dog place was in my budget, but two Dodger games would probably set me back a couple of hundred at least.

"OK, Richard. Thanks again."

I hung up and pulled out my laptop and found the listing for Indiana White Pages. I clicked and then clicked again on reverse phone number look ups. I fed the 8 digit number in and clicked. No known information.

Sometimes it works, sometimes it doesn't.

I called an old friend that I had met shortly after my divorce, and one for whom I had a great deal of respect and admiration still lingering in my old ticker. She was Director of Customer Services for the telephone company in California, and might not have any influence or knowledge of the system in Indiana, but if it dealt with phones, she might know the right people to contact.

After a few pleasantries, she got down to business and put me on hold while she made some phone calls from her office.

"I'm sorry, Kip," she said. My heart sank. She wasn't going to be able to help me.

"I can't help you personally, but I'll give you the number of a person who might be in position to help." I perked up.

She gave me another phone number with an 812 area code, wished me luck and hung up.

I dialed the new number.

"Customer Service, AT&T," a woman's voice.

I gave the scenario to the woman who owned the voice, and waited. She did some clicking and clacking on a computer somewhere across the Wabash from where I sat waiting in Peoria, Illinois, and a few seconds later she came back on the line.

"That number is a cell phone," she said. "I'm sorry, but regulations do not permit me to divulge the name to whom that phone is registered."

"Well, dang it Ma'am," I said, putting on a drawl. "I've got that number as the place that repairs air conditioners, and mine is on the fritz again. Can you tell me the city where it is registered, maybe I'm a few digits off or something."

"It's an Indianapolis number," she said. "I'm sorry, but that is all the information I am permitted to relate." She hung up.

Indianapolis. That's a big place, I thought. I clicked on "search" and typed in "population of Indianapolis" just for the hell of it. I found that 853, 178 people reside in 347 square miles. It is the second largest city in the Midwest next to Chicago and the 14th largest in the nation.

Trying to find out who owned the number Richard had given me would be like pulling hen's teeth or frog hairs.

Well Yardley, I told myself, there's only one way to find out. Dial the danged number.

I dialed it.

"Ford residence," a voice said.

Residence? I was told it was a cell phone. Then it occurred to me that some people have disconnected land lines and use a cell phone with blue tooth hook ups as their home phones.

Nanoseconds later I had registered the name "Ford" and connected it to Marion Ford, one of the big shots at the drug company where the heist had occurred. A second and a half after that I dreamed up what I would say.

"I'm sorry to disturb you, but we have a report of an electrical outage in your area. Can you tell me if it has reached your street?"

"No, the electricity is on here," the voice said.

"Maybe it is on the grid of the next block," I said, sounding official. "Are you on Walnut Street?"

"No, this is Meridian Street."

"In the eighteen hundred block?"

"No, sir. This home is in the twelve hundred block."

"OK." I said. "Sorry to bother you, Ma'am."

"All right. Goodbye."

"Goodbye, and thank you."

The line went dead.

I had information. The number that was written on the wall of one of the trailers used in the drug heist belonged to someone named Ford. Marion Ford, in my mind, and although I didn't know exactly where to find him, I could get close.

I packed an overnight bag and left Peoria in the rented car. It's 192 miles from Peoria to Indianapolis and an easy three and a half hour drive. I stopped once for lunch and gas at a Pilot truck stop and was there by four o:clock.

My intentions had been to get a room in an inexpensive motel, spend the night, then try to contact Marion Ford the next day for an interview. It turned out that no inexpensive motel rooms were available and I wound up staying at a place that was going to set me back nearly two hundred bucks a night. I fully intended to make it a "one night stand".

The next day I found Meridian without any problems and drove until I found the 1200 block. The homes were beautiful. All of them sat back 500 feet or more from the street on landscaped and manicured lawns. Some had white vinyl fence surrounding them making them look like horse ranches. I had no idea which one belonged to Marion Ford, but drove up and down the street looking for mailboxes. Some of the boxes had names on them, I noticed, but none had "Ford" on it. I picked one with the name "Sterling" on it and wrote down the number. It was 1222. I found a shady spot and parked the car, hauled out my laptop and found the Indianapolis white pages. I looked up "Sterling" at 1222 Meridian Lane and found a phone number. I dialed it.

"Sterling residence," a woman's voice.

"Mrs. Sterling?"

"This is the Sterling maid," she said.

"Oh, I'm sorry. I was calling for Mrs. Sterling. Is she there?"

"No," the maid said. "She's not expected back until later this evening. May I help you."

"Is she having dinner with Mrs. Ford?"

"I wouldn't know," she said.

"I guess I could stop by Mrs. Ford's place and see if she can tell me what I need to know," I said. "I represent Greater Indianapolis Garden Club. Mrs. Sterling is in the running for Gardener of the Month."

"I'm unaware of that," the maid said, nonchalantly.

"Isn't Mrs. Ford's home the one with the beautiful Colorado Blue Spruce trees lining the driveway?" I had seen a home like that on Meridian Lane.

"No, that's the Grayson Estate," she said. "The Ford home is the one with the two giant oak trees. It's diagonally across from the Grayson's."

"Oh yes, I see that on my list now, how silly of me!"

"Is there something else?"

"No, I think I can find the information I need now," I said. "Thank you." I clicked the cell phone shut before she could start to wonder about the whole conversation.

The one with the two big oak trees. That should be easy enough. It's diagonally across from the one with the Colorado Spruce trees. That would be 1224 Meridian Lane.

CHAPTER 24

A maid answered the door and for a second I forgot all about the scenario I would make up to get in to see Marion Ford. She was wearing a very tight fitting black jump suit with a zipper up the front. Well, not all the way up. As a matter of fact, it wasn't up at all. The zipper stopped at her belly button. The inside half of each of her magnificent breasts were exposed, along with a lovely span of tummy and a beautiful throat that led to a face that should have been on Avon calendars; the rest of her in Victoria's Secrets calendars.

"Yes," she said.

"Um, yes," I repeated. I stood there trying to think of something to say, but "yes" was what came out.

"May I help you?"

"Yes." I said again. "Yes, yes. Um, I think you can help me. Yes."

She stared at me.

"Are you OK? Do you speak English?"

"Oh, sorry. Yes, I speak English and yes, I'm OK, and yes, I hope you can help me. I'm here to see Marion Ford, is he in?"

"Yes," she said.

I stood there waiting.

She stood there staring at me. I was getting a little uncomfortable. I thought perhaps my fly was open or something.

"Would you please tell Mr. Ford that there's an officer from unsolved cases who wishes to speak with him?"

"Police?" she asked.

"Mmuum." I muttered.

She left me standing and walked away from me with a wiggle that would have been banned from television in the sixties. "Two possums fightin' in a gunny sack," Redd Foxx would have said.

I looked around. The place was neat and well decorated, but I noticed that the furniture all looked as though it had been new in the sixties. Nothing modern, all period furniture, overstuffed divans, square end tables and coffee table, all a dark maple. Pictures hung on the wall in precise manner, not an inch away from symmetric. The paintings were nice, but showed no promise of being high dollar, just paintings. You could buy them at yard sales.

A huge bookcase was against one wall and I walked to it and read some of the titles. Most were mysteries. A complete set of Edgar Allen Poe's works, Erle Stanley Gardner, Ellory Queen. The most recent title I noticed was "Presumed Innocent" by Scott Turow. I guessed that it was published in the mid to late 80's.

I heard a shuffle of feet and turned to see a man in his mid 60's.

"I'm Marion Ford," he said.

His voice was one of those mid to high range. half falsetto, voices that are sometimes associated with homosexuals.

He wore a pair of dark green trousers and a flowered yellow shirt with the initials, MFF embroidered above the pocket. I recognized him from the picture in the book that had cost me twenty bucks at AGC Pharmaceuticals.

I extended my hand and he shook it like a woman picking up a baby chick. I am not fond of men who shake hands like women.

"My name is Yardley, Mr. Ford," I said.

"You are from the police?"

"Actually I'm a private investigator from Los Angles," I said. "I'm working a case regarding the heist at AGC. It occurred to me that you might be able to answer some questions about that case."

"What kind of questions did you have in mind, Mr. Yardley?" he asked. "I've been over that case with the police at least a dozen times, and I'm running late for an appointment."

"You haven't talked to the police lately, though," I interjected. "My main question is this. Why would your phone number turn up in a trailer that may have been used to haul away the drugs heisted from AGC?"

"Your guess is as good as mine, Yardley," he said. "If someone wrote my phone number on a bathroom wall, would that mean I had used that bathroom?"

He smiled at me like he knew what I was thinking. He wasn't far from wrong, I was thinking that is probably where homosexuals would find his phone number.

"Would you remember an employee named Billy Brooks? And when is the last time you had any contact with Billy?"

"I remember Brooks," he said, no sign of any concern on his face. "He worked for me at AGC. I haven't spoken to him since I left the company."

"Are you aware that Billy tried to sell two trailers and spent time in prison for that attempt?"

"No, that isn't something that I would have learned," he said.

"Do you know anything about a suitcase that might have been entrusted to Billy to deliver to you?" I was stretching it a little.

"Nope." he said. "I'm afraid you've come a long way for answers that I don't have, Kip." he said. "Now if you'll excuse me, I have some books to return to the library."

"One more question," I said. "Are you familiar with Cory West?"

"I knew Cory at AGC," he said. "I haven't heard from him either."

"Did you know that Mr. West had obtained employment with an insurance investigating firm and was assigned to investigate the claim filed by AGC after the heist?"

"No, I did not know that," he said. "What does all of this have to do with me, Kip? I've been retired since I left AGC, and know nothing about the proceedings regarding the "heist" as you call it."

"So there's no reason someone would have written your phone number in a trailer that may have been used in that heist? No reason you can think of?" I was trying to bait him, let him think about a reason that only he might know.

"None." he said.

"OK, thank you for your time, Mr. Ford."

I turned as if to leave.

"Will you let me know if you find an answer?" he asked.

"Sure," I said. "I'll keep in touch."

I left the big house and headed for the rental in the driveway. Something just didn't seem right about Marion Ford. I was careful to watch his face when he answered my questions, and I'm a pretty good judge of expressions. His expression never changed during our conversation. Yet the feeling that he was lying persisted in my old brain cells. If there's one thing I've learned to trust in my tenure of P.I. work, it is my instinct.

Back in the car, I sat for a moment thinking about Ford's maid. She seemed pleasant enough, and my manly thoughts began to ramble. "Knock it off, Yardley," I told myself, started the engine and drove away. It was going to be a long drive back to Peoria, Pig Capitol of the World. As I drove away, I finally realized what had been bothering me. It seemed to me like Ford had been expecting me. Something he said, just a feeling. One, he didn't ask me for identification. Two, he had called me "Kip" twice during our talk. I didn't tell him my first name.

That left a couple of possibilities. Either someone had talked to him about me prior to my trip to Indianapolis, or he had a way to identify people, perhaps by taking photos of them without their knowledge, and running them through a computer to see if it matched any picture that had ever been posted. I know my picture had been posted in news columns on the internet, and maybe that's how it happened.

But I had the strange feeling that someone had tipped off Marion Ford that I was in route even before I left Peoria.

Then I started doubting myself. Kip is an unusual name. My father had read a poem by Rudyard Kipling in high school, then a story by Kipling about a young lad who wanted to be a spy. The lad's name was Kip. So that's how I became

Rudyard Kipling Yardley. Had I told the maid that my name was Kip Yardley? If so, maybe she told Ford. I ran through the conversation with her to the best of my memory and couldn't decide if I had told her my full name or not.

I decided to backtrack and ask the maid. Ford had said he was leaving and that would be a chance to talk to the maid undisturbed. I had only driven five or six miles, and I wasn't in any real hurry to get back to Peoria, so I turned the car around and headed back to 1224 Meridian Lane, Indianapolis, Indiana. Home of the Colts. Home of the Indy 500.

CHAPTER 25

Through the screen she said, "Yes?"

"I just wondered about something," I said. "When I was here before, did I tell you who I am?"

"No," she said. "Do I need to know?"

"I didn't tell you my name?"

"No, you did not. Was there something else?"

"How did you announce to Mr. Ford that I was here?"

"You told me you were an officer from unsolved cases, I believe," she said. "Now if there's nothing else, I have work to do."

"Oh." I said. "Well, may I speak to Mrs. Ford?"

"Sir, there is no Mrs. Ford. She died about 10 years ago. I've been employed as Mr. Ford's maid since then."

"I see," I said.

"Where is the library?" I asked. She told me it was a mile and a half back up Meridian Street.

I headed the rented car back up Meridian, looking for a library. As I neared the library building I saw a police car fall in behind me from a side street. I parked the car in the library parking lot and started in. Two uniformed officers sat in a cruiser that parked next to my car.

I get a strange feeling when police officers park next to my car. They are generally not there to protect my vehicle. Inside the library, I walked to a window where I could see my car and the squad car. The officers were still there, sitting in their car.

I looked all around the first floor of the library and did not see Marion Ford. If he had planned to visit the library that morning, he had either made a quick trip in and out or else he was in the upstairs portion, browsing bookshelves. I took the stairs to the open deck above and made a quick pass at the end of the shelves, looking down the aisles. No one was there.

The librarian was no help. She told me that she doesn't watch everyone who comes and goes. When I asked if Marion Ford had a library card she got huffy and told me that their patrons privacy policy was strictly enforced. I knew that showing her my PI badge wouldn't help, so I left.

The squad car was gone. I breathed a sigh of relief. Whatever they wanted perhaps didn't involve me. Maybe it had something to do with the rented car I was driving. But as I reached the next signal light I saw blue lights flashing in my rearview mirror and realized that something was up.

I pulled to the side of the street at the first opportunity and sure enough, the police car pulled in behind me.

I waited. A tall cop approached the driver's side door, his right hand resting on his Glock. I waited some more. He tapped on the window and I could hear his deep bass voice instructing me to turn off the engine and roll down the window. I complied.

"What's the problem, Officer?" I asked.

"Drivers license and registration, please."

"This is a rental, the registration is in the glove compartment," I said, knowing that a rookie cop might take a move towards the glove box as an effort to haul out a weapon. I didn't feel like being riddled with 9MM this morning.

"Open it," he said.

I opened the glove box door and retrieved the registration and handed it to him. "My driver's license is from California," I said, "It's in my wallet, left front pocket."

"OK," he said. "Get it."

I got it and handed it to him. Good thing I had left the 9MM in my motel room.

"Step out of the car, Mr. Yardley," he said. "Please put your hands on your head when you are out."

I followed instructions. Must be serious, I thought.

"Would you mind telling me what is up?"

"We have a 'seek and detain' warrant. You are wanted in Illinois for questioning regarding the death of a man named Brooks."

"Billy Brooks?" I asked. "I didn't even know he was dead."

"My partner will drive your vehicle to the station, Sir," he said. "Please come with me."

Polite guy.

I followed him to the squad car and waited while he opened the back door, I got in quickly. I wasn't handcuffed, as is the procedure when someone is taken in for questioning. This entire scenario wasn't good. I was going to spend a day or two in lock up until someone either came and got me from Illinois, or one of Indiana's State Troopers took me to Illinois. In either case, I was going to be incapacitated for a while, and I had spent enough time on this case. Things were dragging and it was time to either fish or cut bait. Looks like I'm not going to be able to do either for a while.

CHAPTER 26

It was late the next day when I put in my "one" phone call. I called Toby Smith at the California Highway Patrol office. An Illinois State Trooper had arrived and brought a driver to drive my rental. I was now in the custody of Peoria, IL's law enforcement.

"What's up?" he asked.

"I need some help," I said.

"Where are you, and what kind of help?"

"I'm in Peoria as a guest of their finest law enforcement hotel."

"In jail?"

"Yep. I was arrested on suspicion. A warrant for killing the guy that throws people to the hogs."

"Don't say stuff like that," he said. "I'm not supposed to even know about that incident, and this might not be a secure line."

"Sorry," I said.

"So you are in for suspension of murder?"

"You got it. Can you get me out on my own recognizance?"

"Have they set bail? How much money are we talking about here, and where do you suggest I find the money?"

"Ten grand." I said. "I've got the money in my savings at the bank. It can be wired here if they'll let me call the bank. Problem is, I need someone to appear on my behalf as a witness to my character."

"And that someone is? Rhonda, maybe?"

"I was thinking of her," I said. "But the person I'd like to see show up is talking to me."

"Me?" Silence.

I waited.

I waited some more.

"Yes, Toby." I said. "You would be the best witness for my character that I can think of. I don't know any priests, and even if I did, I'm not Catholic, so I haven't been to confession."

"When?" I knew he was thinking about it.

"Tomorrow." I said. "One in the afternoon."

"Damn. That means I'll have to get out of here on a flight tonight. You sure give a guy advance notice when you need help," he said, sarcastically.

"I'd do the same for you," I said.

"I don't think I've ever been arrested for suspicion of murder," he said. "Furthermore, I don't intend to."

"Come on, Toby, be a pal."

More silence.

Finally. "All right, Kip," he said. "I'll be there. Should I bring my clubs so we can make it pleasure after business?"

"I don't have mine," I said, "But if you want to go by my place and get them, bring them. We can take time to play."

"Too much hassle," he said. "I'd like to, but I'll just book the next flight back. I can get away for a day or two without raising any eyebrows around CHP but if I stayed and played golf I might get in trouble. What if I made a hole in one back there? Who could I tell?"

"OK," I said. "Golf when this is done. I'm getting a strange feeling about this case, and I'm anxious to end it, with or without the fifty grand fee."

"That's your problem, Kip. You always fall for those huge offers then you get stuck on cases you really don't want to be on. Settle for divorce cases and missing teens and you'll make more money and get to stay home more. Any ideas on how to tie that one up?"

"Not yet, Toby." I had some ideas, but they were not clear in my mind, so I figured I'd keep them to myself.

"OK, Kip." He said. "See you tomorrow. Wear your best suit."

He knew I probably would be dressed in Levis and tee shirt, or something very casual.

He knew me.

CHAPTER 27

Toby was there just as he said he'd be. He didn't come to visit me in my opulent room, with hot and cold running water, fresh laundered sheets and pillow cases, a chocolate mint on the bed pillow. Yeah, right.

The court appearance for my release went well. by two that afternoon I was out and eating lunch with Toby at a Cracker Barrel. He loved big breakfasts, and since there were no Cracker Barrels in California, he wanted to go to one while he was in the Midwest.

We talked between bites, I gave him a rundown on where I was and why I was in Indianapolis. He didn't offer any suggestions. He rarely does. Police investigations take totally different turns sometimes. Forensic evidence, finger prints, witnesses, time consuming collection of data, all play a part when the cops do it. Private investigators have a reputation for cutting red tape, busting a few heads, breaking and entering when needed, hiding evidence until it can solve a case, and a few hundred other tricks of the trade that Toby knew I would use. He also knew I didn't kill anyone unless that person was trying to kill me.

He had a plane to catch and I had a long drive back to Peoria, so we said our goodbyes over a beer at the airport.

It was nearly dark when I got back to my motel. I could smell the corn as I drove through the county. The smell of corn when it tassels has always been a favorite of mine. It brought back memories of when I was fourteen and worked cutting the tassels off of the stalks.

Once I had worked for two days, 16 hours, for fifty cents an hour. Then the guy who hired me tried to stiff me. I went to his office twice for my money and he kept putting me off with "come back Monday" or "come back Friday". I finally told my Dad.

"Get in the car," Dad said. I knew the shit was going to hit the fan.

At the office, Dad didn't waste any time.

"My boy says he worked for you for two days and you haven't paid him."

"Oh he'll get paid when I get paid," the man said.

"No. He'll get paid right now," Dad said. "If you don't have $8 on you, I'll wait until you go to the bank

and get it. But if you don't come back within an hour, I'll hunt you down and it'll cost a lot more than $8 to repair your teeth."

I got my $8.

Later there was an article in the paper about the guy trying to screw all of the boys he had hired. Here's one kid who didn't get screwed, thanks to Dad.

I parked the rental in the motel lot and after carefully checking my door, I got in the room and took a hot shower, put on some clean clothes and had supper in the restaurant. There wasn't anything worth watching on TV so I read the paper.

Billy had been found dead in his room. He hadn't shown up for his court appearance, so police had went there with a warrant. He had been shot in the back of the head and was sprawled half on and half off of the cot. The room had been ransacked.

Local police had found my prints in his room and a warrant was issued. How the police knew I was in Indianapolis was not explained. Whatever he had known about suitcases, hog feeding, or drug heists, would never be disclosed. As I thought of that, it occurred to me that perhaps he had been killed because he knew too much.

I wondered how he got out of jail so fast. It had only been six days since I hauled his butt in to Donahue. I made a mental note to check with the bail bondsmen around the courthouse to see who had bailed him out.

I was just about to drift off to sleep when my phone rang. It was Donahue.

"Got some news, Yardley," he said.

"Billy?"

"You guessed it." He sounded like I should have been surprised.

"What else is new?" I asked. "This case is getting stranger every day. I spent a couple of days in lock up because of Billy's demise, now you're telling me he's dead. I knew that day before yesterday."

"That aint all that's new," he said. "We found your phone."

"The one Billy threw in the river?"

"That's the one," he said. "Divers found it yesterday. We've got technicians on it to see if any data is salvageable. "

"Can I have it back? I know a guy back home who can get info from it, even if it has been burned and ran through a concrete mixer."

"Sorry, no can do. It's evidence, and we'll just have to wait for our boys to examine it."

"What'll that do for me?" I asked.

"Well, if we find what you told me on there, it might help you in the State's case against you for killing Billy."

"You know I didn't kill Billy," I said. "I had no reason to. Besides, if I'd wanted Billy dead he would have drowned in the same river where he tried to drown me. I don't work like that."

"Didn't think you did that job," he said. "But then, we have to take it step by step, and your prints were found there. What the hell were you thinking going there? What did you expect to find?"

"Who knows?" I said. "Hell, I've found stuff that didn't mean a thing when I found it, later turns out it was key to the case I was working. I just try to cover all bases."

"Speaking of bases, I've got a game tomorrow. We need a guy who can play second base. There'll be plenty of dames and more beer than we can drink. Interested?"

I thought about it. It had been a while since I'd played softball, but I really liked the game and this case was getting to me. I needed some time away, and it might be fun to get out in the sunshine, get some exercise, drink a cool one or two, and enjoy the day.

"Where? What time?" I asked.

"Bielfeldt Park, Peoria Heights, one o'clock."

"I don't know, Donahue," I said. "I don't have a uniform or a glove. Unless I can play in Levis and you can loan me a glove."

"It's a practice game. I've got a half a dozen gloves, and you can wear your skivvies as far as I'm concerned."

"Oh I guess I can stand the exercise," I said.

"Good. Know how to find the place?"

"I'll find it," I said.

"Good," he repeated. "See you there at about 12:30, infield and batting practice."

"All right." I said. "See you."

I hung up and turned on the television to watch a Cardinals baseball game. The idea of playing softball helped ease the tension of being arrested, under suspicion of murder, man eating hogs, suitcases, cell phone evidence, and a million other things that I had on my mind.

CHAPTER 28

Early the next morning I was up, showered, had breakfast and looked up the location of the softball field, before I got the call.

It was from Richard Rheams.

"What's cooking, you still looking?"

"Hello Richard." I said. "Your name should have been Richard Rhymes." I had known him long enough to know that he always tries to rhyme his greetings. He talks in rhymes and probably dreams and thinks in rhymes. He's probably the most valuable source of help I've ever had in solving my cases.

"I've got something I need to tell you, do you want it now or when you get back?"

"Give it to me."

"Not hardly, Kip Yardley," he said. "This is big. It'll cost you, like, three dinners, a Laker game, a Dodger game and maybe a trip to the World Series."

I thought about that. The money wasn't the big thing, it was the time I'd have to sit next to Richard at those events, and listen to him analyze the game in his sing-song, poetry spouting, rhyming way. I liked the guy, but sometimes he drove me nuts.

"How big is it?"

"Bigger than a bread box, White Sox."

"OK, Richard," I sighed. "Give it to me."

"You know that piece of metal you sent me?"

"Yeah..the one with the phone number? Thank you, Richard, that was good work."

"There's more, three four, open the door."

"What?" I asked, surprised.

"I happened to look at the flip side of that album, good buddy. There was a tiny little piece of green paper stuck to it. Of course my analytical mind wanted to know what that piece of green paper stuck to the flip side might be, you see."

"Of course," I agreed. "What was it?"

"Money."

"Money?" I was thinking it might have stuck to a dollar bill I had in my pocket the day I cut it from the trailer. "What kind of money?"

"From my analysis, I'd say a large denomination piece of US currency."

My heart went from zero to sixty in one hundredth of a second.

"How large?"

"I'm not sure," he said. "In comparison to other US currency notes, however, I'd say it was at least a fifty dollar bill, probably more like a hundred."

"You can tell that by analyzing a scrap of paper?"

"Currency of this country is printed on special paper, as you know, Kip," he said. "Each denomination has a different process involved in making that paper. It is just a matter of analyzing the chemicals in the paper to see what denomination the bill is."

"You haven't done that yet?" I asked.

"No, I'm going to start that this morning. Just thought you'd like to know the news, St. Louis Blues."

"I do, and thank you," I said.

"You're welcome, Malcom."

"Cut it out, Shakespeare, your killing my ear."

He laughed and hung up.

I started wondering why a piece of a large denomination bill would be stuck to the back of a piece of metal I had cut from the wall of a 40 foot cargo trailer. There were many ways it might have happened. The piece might have been on the metal when the trailer was built, it might have been placed there as a marker, or some kind of clue as to the whereabouts of the drug sales money. Maybe there was a map or directions on that wall that I had overlooked.

I decided I'd go take another look at the trailer after the softball game.

***

I got to the ballpark just as the practice started. Donahue met me in the parking lot and led me back to his car where he popped the trunk.

"Take your pick," he said, motioning to a bunch of softball gloves. I looked them over and picked up a couple, flexed them to see if they were stiff or flexible enough for an infielder's mitt. I chose one.

"I'm ready," I said. "Let's get this show on the road."

We walked to a group of men standing next to home plate. Donahue yelled at them.

"Listen up! This is Kip Yardley, a friend of mine recommended him to me to play second base today." He went around the group of men introducing each one by their first names only. I wouldn't remember half of them, but I tried to place them in my memory bank by associating them with their looks.

"OK," Donahue said. "Let's take our positions and get some infield in. I'll hit some grounders."

A tall, thin guy with gray hair stood behind the plate to take throws back from the fielders. Donahue dumped an armload of softballs behind the thin guy and tossed one up and hit it to the first baseman. The first baseman scooped it up, and fired it home. Thin man caught it and flipped another ball to

Donahue and he hit it hard on the ground and to my left. I moved left and got in front of it, it hit the heel of the glove and trickled off towards right field. I felt stupid but ran after the ball and picked it up and threw it home.

"S'allright, Kip," Donahue yelled. "Again."

He hit another one to my right and I moved that way, leaned across my body and fielded the hard hit grounder, and fired the ball home.

"That's better," he yelled.

And so the infield practice continued, with the customary ground balls around the horn, some double play grounders, and some pop ups. Donahue then whistled and hit a liner to left. The fielder grabbed it nicely on the first hop and threw a liner to me. I caught it, pivoted, and threw it home.

"Nice throw, Kip," Donahue yelled.

After ten minutes of infield practice Donahue hit a grounder to first who fielded it, threw home and followed it in. I was next. A slow roller right of the mound. I fielded it, threw it home and followed the first baseman to the dugout. The play continued around the horn.

"You're pretty good," the first baseman said.

"Haven't played in awhile," I said.

"Well if your half the second baseman as you are private detective, you'll do fine."

That statement left me curious. Had Donahue told these guys about me?

"Don't believe everything you hear," I said, laughing. "Donahue might not know me that well."

"He's been talking you up since Drake hurt his elbow and we thought of replacing him," he said.

"Drake's elbow will heal. He'll be back."

"He hurt in back in April," the first baseman said. "We've heard nothing but good things about you since then."

That made me curious. I didn't even know Donahue in April.

"Donahue was ringing my bell?" I asked.

"Yeah. He was telling us about a L.A. private eye who had solved some pretty good cases. Said he'd like to have you on his side of the badge as well as on the softball team."

Now I was really confused. Donahue had talked about me and some of the cases I had worked long before I even took the suitcase caper.

"Ah, he was probably just blowing steam," I said.

"Yeah, come to think of it, it was the night we all went out before our first game. It was a second celebration of winning the championship last year. He might have been a little tipsy."

I didn't say anything. Maybe Donahue had heard about my cases from Toby Smith. I decided I would call Toby after the game and ask him.

Once the game started, I forgot all about the conversation that had taken place with the first baseman in the dugout. We played a really good defensive game and I singled with a man on second to score our only run. We lost 2-1. I felt good about the game and the way I had played.

"Good game, you guys," Donahue told us. "We'll get them next time. We played good on defense. Just need to quit trying for the fences with the bats. OK, let's have a beer or two."

There were no other games scheduled for that field so we sat in the dugout, drank beer and told war stories, I'm a little reserved to talk about my personal life, but after two or three beers I was asked about my marital status. Most of the guys were married. Donahue, myself, and Daryl, the tall graying man who had caught infield practice, were all single. The jokes started flowing like water, or rather like beer. I laughed so hard I was hurting.

"Well, thanks for letting me play with you guys," I said, "If I'm around, I'll play again, if you'll have me."

"Where you going?" Someone asked.

"Back to LA, as soon as I wrap up this case I'm on now."

"We'll talk about that later, Kip," Donahue said.

I shook hands all around, told them what a great bunch of guys they were, and left. There was something I was going to do, but the beer had made me a little unsure of what it was that was bugging me. I was not even close to being under the influence, and felt completely sober enough to drive. Three beers was about my limit in most cases unless I had someone else driving.

I took the expressway back to my motel, parked the car and went to my room and showered. By the time I got dressed I was hungry so I headed for the dining room of the motel, and completely forgot about calling Toby Smith until I was back in my room, watching a golf tournament on television.

I punched in Toby's home phone number and went to the mini-fridge for a beer.

"Hello, Toby Smith here."

"Hi Toby, it's me."

"What are you up to, Kip? Shot anyone lately?"

"Not since the last time," I said. "I wanted to ask you a question. When did you tell Donahue about me?"

"When you talked to me about seeing who was in charge of the old drug heist."

"Not before then?"

"Nope. Why?"

"I played ball with his team today and one of the guys said Donahue had praised my detecting skills back in April. I was just curious how he knew anything about me prior to you talking to him."

"I didn't say very much," Toby said. "Just that you were working a case and could use his help."

"Hmmm. That's pretty weird. Why did he know anything about me prior to that?"

"Don't know, Kip," he said. "Are you sure the guy you talked to had his dates right?"

"He mentioned a specific date, back in April."

"Well, your guess is as good as mine. I don't know Donahue real well, just played against him in the championship police officers slow pitch tournament. We had a banquet dinner and I sat next to him. We talked. That's about all I know."

"OK, Toby. Thanks."

That was weird.

Somehow or another Donahue had heard about me before I had taken the gig at Sanders pool party. And Sanders seemed to know a lot about me when he hired me. I was beginning to think the two of them had talked and that they had did some research on me. I was getting a little homesick for LA and Rhonda was constantly popping up in my mind so I decided to take a break and fly back to LA. I intended to make a trip to Sanders computer store and ask him what his connection might be to Donahue.

CHAPTER 29

The airplane had no sooner touched down in LAX when I woke up. I guess it was the little bump when the wheels hit the ground. I normally will wake up at the sound of the landing gear doors opening and the gear going down, but I had driven to the Peoria airport after dinner on the day I played the ball game, anxious to see Rhonda. Fortunately the flight to LA was wide open and I didn't have a problem getting on. Denver was crowded as usual when we topped there. An hour layover gave me time to grab a sandwich and beer, and I had fallen asleep right after takeoff. Now I was groggy as the aircraft taxied to the terminal in Los Angeles.

It was only 8:30 in LA. I called Rhonda.

Her phone rang a couple of times before she answered.

"Hello."

"Hi Rhonda," I said. "I just got in to LA. Are you busy?"

"Not too busy for you," she said. "Did you finish your work in Peoria?"

"Unfortunately, no," I said. "I just need a break and I was missing you. Can I come over?"

"Sure," she said. "I'm at the mall, but I can be home before you get there. Have you eaten?"

"Yes, I had a sandwich in Denver. I just want to nibble on you for dessert."

She laughed. "I hope you are good and hungry, then."

We chatted a few minutes and said goodbyes and I picked up my Caddy in the long term parking lot and headed for her home in Long Beach. The traffic around the airport wasn't heavy and soon thinned out on the 405 south. It felt good to be home. I had thought about stopping somewhere and buying some flowers but I realized that most places would be closed and my desire to see Rhonda was growing stronger every time the odometer in the Caddy clicked another tenth of a mile.

There are parts of every story that should never be told. What Rhonda and I did when I got to her house is that part. I'll just say that dessert was good.

She had already left the house when I woke up. There was a note on the coffee pot that read, "Glad you were hungry. Call me."

I poured a cup of coffee and drank it. She had left a slice of banana bread out for me and I ate that. Then I found my way to her bedroom and got a pair of Dockers from her closet. I leave a few clothes at her house for purposes like this one when I unexpectedly spend the night. I took the clothes to the bathroom with me, shaved with an old razor I had left in her medicine cabinet, showered and dressed. I wrote her a little note under her note. "Thanks for dessert."

The drive back to my apartment was uneventful, traffic was heavy. I stopped and gathered my mail, sorted it, tossed the junk mail and left the good stuff and bills on the counter in the kitchen. I had a second cup of coffee while I riffled through the mail, then put the cup in the sink and left for Semi Valley to see Sanders.

It never fails that when you are thinking of ways a case is going, you will almost always stop and go over everything in your mind several times, adding little bits here and eliminating little bits there. The radio was on and I was absent mindedly listening to the stock report. The analyst was saying something about "both buyers and sellers had something to gain in early trading this morning, as is reflected by the early morning Wall Street numbers ...."

That's when it dawned on me that all of my attention so far on this case had revolved around the theft of pharmaceuticals and the sale thereof. I realized that there might be a lot more to learn if I started snooping around on the other end, the folks that purchased the stolen pharmaceuticals. I was deep in thought on that subject for my drive to Simi Valley and had almost arrived at Saunders computer shop without much conscious effort.

Someone had been waiting with a big bundle of cash to buy the drug heist. Who? How would I go about finding anything regarding the buyers? At first it seemed like an insurmountable task, but I decided to dig around in some library archives, make calls to some old friends, and see if I could stir up anything. I diverted my destination and drove to an older part of Simi Valley where I knew I would find a library. If I was lucky they might have articles or tidbits from the Florida coast or the Louisiana, Alabama area, regarding drug purchases, drug busts, or other items that might yield a lead.

I found some reference books on pharmaceuticals that had been busted about 8 years prior for illegal sales of prescription drugs, namely oxycondone and percodan. One caught my attention, as it had gone public the year after the drug heist, and had been shut down eighteen months after the drug heist. Estimates were in the 100 million dollar range as to their profits over the 18 month period. I decided to check that one first.

I put in a call to a detective named Happs who worked in the Homestead area, and who had been in charge of a murder investigation I had solved a year before. Happs was glad to hear from me, but had little information that was useful. I hung up and called a man who knew more about the ins and outs of Florida profiteering than anyone I could think of. His name is Charles DuPont. He is the great grandfather of a beautiful girl who inherited a 114 million dollar lotto ticket that I found after her mother lost her life on a Florida beach.

I got DuPont's manservant and waited until the vibrant voice came alive in my phone.

"Charles DuPont," he said.

"Good morning, Sir," I said. "I hope I didn't disturb you."

"Is this Kip Yardley?"

"Yes, Mr. DuPont," I said, glad that he recognized my voice.

"Hello," he said, sounding glad to hear from me. "How can I be of service, Kip?"

"I'm seeking some information regarding a pharmaceutical company that went public about 10 years ago, made a fortune selling pain killers, then was shut down by the State of Florida for some dealings with a notorious pill pushing operation."

"Let me guess," he said. "You're speaking of Florpharma Corporation?"

"Exactly. Do you know much about them?"

"What is it you wish to know?" he asked.

"Board of Directors? Key players?"

"They were headed by a middle aged woman whose name is Martha Downing. She avoided jail time by a plea bargain, claiming she knew nothing of the second hand sales the pain killers went through."

"Downing? Doesn't match with anything I've got here," I said. "Was that a married name or maiden name, do you know?"

"Probably maiden. I don't think she was married at that time, although she may have married later."

"Description?"

"I'll have some people do some research, Kip. Then I'll fax everything I know to you. OK?"

"That'll be fine, Mr. DuPont. Thanks for your time. I owe you one."

We chatted for a few minutes, I thanked him for the information he had provided, although I wasn't sure what, if anything, it meant to the case I was currently trying to solve. He promised to fax details to my office in California when they became available. We said our goodbyes and I hung up.

There were things that were starting to make sense in the case, but nothing was rattling the old brain cells yet. I find that the older I get the more time it takes me to recognize relevant factors in my work. Maybe it is time to hang up the PI badge and settle down.

I drove back to the strip mall where Sanders had his computer repair business and sat in the lot watching the door for several minutes. I don't know what I was watching for, but I had nothing with which to confront Sanders, and sat thinking about what I was going to say to him. He had ruffled my feathers on our last meeting, and I had left with a warning to him that if he double crossed me no one would help pull his crippled ass out of the swimming pool the next time he was drowning. I guess I could go in and see if I could smooth things out a little, bring him up to date on my search for the elusive suitcase, and see if he had anything that might help me find it.

He looked up from a work bench as I entered his shop.

"Yardley." He said. "Any news?"

"Hello, Sanders," I said. "I haven't found your suitcase, if that's what you are asking."

"That was my primary concern," he said, sounding as if he had forgot all about our last meeting.

"I've been nearly drowned, knocked colder than yesterday's pizza, locked up and threatened," I said. "And I have nothing to show for it. A lot of clues, maybe, but nothing firm. The question I have is this. Can you tell me what's in the suitcase?"

"What do you think?"

"Money, I've been told." I said.

"Who told you that?"

"Billy." I watched his face. He glanced away and back at me rapidly.

"Billy who?"

"I think you know who I'm talking about," I said. "Billy Brooks. You remember him, don't you?

A shipping clerk at the place where you used to work? A drug warehouse that suffered a hundred million dollar burglary?"

"Brooks...Oh. I remember a kid named Brooks. That was a long time ago."

"Well Billy Brooks is dead," I said, watching his face carefully again.

"Dead?"

His reaction was one of surprise and puzzlement. A curious look appeared on his sun-tanned face.

"Any idea who killed him?"

"I didn't say he was murdered," I said quickly.

"No, you didn't." He turned on the workbench chair and used his arms to lift himself to his wheelchair. "It surprised me to learn that he's dead. I just assumed that since you have talked to him and questioned him about the location of the suitcase, that someone else has also found that trail."

"I didn't question him, he questioned me." I said. "I found that he had lived in the place I searched for the suitcase. I talked to his wife, then he showed up in my motel room, hid behind the door and bonked me a good one. He handcuffed me and tried to get me to tell him where the suitcase is. Of course I didn't know, I thought he might know. He pushed me in a river, my hands handcuffed behind me. I'll admit, there was a time when I wanted to kill him, but when the tables were turned, I couldn't push him in the same river. Instead I turned him over to the Peoria police department. A detective named

Donahue who is working the drug warehouse cold case file. Know him?"

"Donahue? No, I don't think I know anyone from back home with that name."

"For some reason, I think you do know him," I told him. He appeared to grimace a little when I said it.

"What makes you say that?"

"Well, it turns out that Donahue knew all about me, my record as a PI, my career with the CHP. A lot about me that he talked to people about before I even took this case. That's why I think you knew him. I think you had him check me out before you hired me."

He pushed controls on his wheel chair and spun it around to face me.

I stepped one step closer, close enough that I could have slapped him hard across his face. But I didn't.

"As a matter of fact, the last words you said before you offered to hire me were ' I probably know a lot more about you than you think I do.'. Do you remember saying that?"

"I don't know what you're talking about," he said smugly. "I paid you the 5G that I promised, if you didn't find the suitcase, so why don't you just turn around and haul your Private Eye ass out of my shop, and we'll forget the whole deal.."

"It's not that easy," I said, "The contract we signed leaves the deal open. There's no time limit on finding the suitcase, and collecting the balance of 45G's. There's no time limit on murder, either."

"You think I killed Billy?"

"No, you probably didn't." I said. "You probably know who did, though. And I'm telling you here, now and up straight, I'm investigating this case and don't intend to quit until I've satisfactorily solved it. If you get tough with me, or send someone to get tough with me, you won't need a suitcase, you'll need a coffin. Got that?"

"Get out, Yardley. Come back with the suitcase and I'll give you the 45G. Otherwise, stay the hell away from me."

"Your choice," I said. "But it occurs to me that if you really want me to find that suitcase, you'll be honest and open with my investigation. Apparently finding the suitcase has fallen off of your "to-do" list. At least it's moved down in urgency."

I turned and walked out of his shop. Now I was damned near certain that for some reason, Donahue and Sanders were in the same boat.

I was beginning to see a glimmer. Someone had one purpose for me. To lead them to the money.

CHAPTER 30

After spending a few days catching up on what my agency was doing, relaxing with Rhonda when she was not working, and thinking about the case of the missing suitcase, I decided it was time to head back to Peoria, the pig capitol of the world.

An uneventful flight back, another car rental, and a change of motels left me in a better mood. I was relaxing poolside at a Holiday Inn a little further from the airport traffic and noise of jets taking off and landing, when I got a call from Donahue.

"Hey, second base," he said. "I just heard you were back in town. Can you drop by my office? My guys found your cell phone, and we'd like to give it back to you."

"Did you clean it up and make it work?"

"Well, since you had made copies of the scene where Billy dumps Cory, we didn't think it was necessary to expense a lot of money and effort to clean up your phone. It's just like we found it, pig poop and all."

"Thanks a bunch, Donahue," I said. "Anything on the case I'm working that you might want to talk to me about?"

"Naw..not really," he said. "As a matter of fact, I was hoping you might have something to tell me, in that regards."

I wanted to ask him what his connection to Sanders was, but bit my tongue and decided that I'd run through my notes before confronting him with that problem.

"How's the team doing?" I asked.

"We could have used you," he said. "Our old second baseman just isn't as sharp as he used to be. If he wasn't a good friend of a lady friend of mine, I would ask you to take his place."

"No thanks, Donahue," I said. "I'm getting too old to play that game on a regular basis. I could hardly walk for two days after playing the last time. I used muscles I haven't used in a while. Besides, I don't intend to stay in Peoria forever."

"Well, stop by and get your phone. Maybe we can have a bite at the spot where my friends hang out, I'll buy you a Bud. By the way, I never thanked you for the cases you brought me. Thanks."

"When would be a good time to come by?"

"Today, say around 12:30?"

"OK. See you then."

I clicked the call end button and rolled off of the chaise lounge and got to my feet. I hadn't told anyone what day I was coming back to Peoria, and as far as I knew, I was the only one who would have known that information. "I just heard you were back in town" was what Donahue had said. I was curious as to what sources he had that were watching my movements. Maybe the same ones who informed Marion Ford that I was headed to Indianapolis?

In my room, I dressed in some Levis and a polo shirt, a pair of Sperry boat shoes and wondered what my next move would be. I dug out a notebook I had been keeping, and when I opened it I saw the newspaper clipping that had fallen from a phone book in Billy Brook's room the night before someone put a slug in Billy's head.

I picked it up and read it. It was the usual pre-auction stuff, city property that was no longer used, confiscated police items, a few vehicles, a lot of jewelry, some furniture, some office equipment. Down near the bottom I saw something that grabbed me like a big bass hitting a rubber minnow.

"Two forty foot trailers made by Fruehauf. These are aluminum skinned trailers that have been in storage for 8 years. No warranty as to highway safety, no inspection certificates. Trailers must be moved at buyers expense. Tires are inflated but not guaranteed they will survive transporting the trailers to another location. This is a final auction. Buyer will provide personal check, bank letter of credit, or cashier's check at time of purchase."

The trailers where I had found Marion Ford's phone number.

A bell went off in my head. On the back of the piece of aluminum that I had cut from one of the trailers, my rhyming jargon friend, Richard Rheames, had discovered a piece of paper that he identified as a fragment of a U.S. Treasury note.

I wondered if Donahue was aware that the trailers were going to be auctioned off, decided to ask him about it when I picked up my cell phone. For now, I had to find out more about the auction. The date in the article for the auction was tomorrow, August 12th. Somehow I needed to either stall that sale date, or buy the trailers and have them hauled to a spot where I could take the inner skin away near the spot where I'd found Marion Ford's number.

I had no idea how much that type of trailer would go for at auction, and briefly wondered if I had enough money in my agency's account to buy it, and to pay for having it moved. Another problem, where the hell was I supposed to move it to?

I got in the car and drove to the impound lot. The trailers were still there in the same spot. The tired old watchman remembered me and waved me in with a salute. I parked next to the one with a hole in the front inner skin, left there the last time I was here, when I sawed out a little chunk. I'd had tools that day.

The tools that I had used were back safely in my office in California, and I really had no idea what I was looking for, but the urge to take a closer look at that trailer was like taking a second bite of coconut cream pie, irresistible. I swung the back doors open and climbed in. There was nothing different about the inside of the trailer. It appeared exactly as I had left it. I took a small LED flashlight and tried to see down inside the skin through the hole I had cut, but to no avail. Without a mirror, or removing a large chunk of skin, I couldn't see a thing.

I got back in the rental and drove to Donahue's office, arriving shortly before the time I had told him I'd be there.

"Kip, the second baseman!" He said.

"Donahue," I replied. "The coach."

"Have a seat," he said. "What's new in the world of Private Eye work?"

"Maybe you can tell me," I said. "Like, how did you find me so fast and who told you I was back in town? I didn't tell anyone I would be back today, and the motel I chose isn't the same one I was in last time here."

"Ah, shit, Kip. Is that all that's bothering you? I'm a cop, remember? I get paid to keep track of people. Particularly people who are nosing around on cold cases that I am in charge of, so to speak."

"Someone who knows what I'm doing, then." I said. "Someone I've talked to about the case? That rules out a whole bunch of people, Donahue. I've talked to about six people here in Peoria, and you are one of them."

"What difference does it make? To quote a famous Secretary of State."

"The difference is this, Donahue. I know a guy in California named Sanders. He's a crippled guy who used to work for the pharmaceutical company. I think he's the one who told you I was coming back. I think you and him combined to bring me here. Maybe I'm as good as you think I am, or maybe I'm not, but I haven't found any suitcase."

"OK," he said. "You got me. I joined forces with Sanders because I wanted to get the top PI available. He called me and asked if I knew anyone who was smart enough to help find a suitcase that he thinks has the payoff cash in it. The two of us screened about twenty guys, me here, and him there, and we chose you. You ought to feel honored. We figured you could solve this case in a week."

"So you're telling me Sanders is on the up and up? That he's not just in it for the bucks?"

"What bucks?"

"Whatever bucks are in the suitcase."

"All I know is my bosses are on my ass to get the case solved, and when he called and offered me money to help find the best PI, I decided to give him a hand. What his motive is, other than the money I don't have the foggiest idea. If he's connected, he'll go down when the case is solved."

"OK" I said. "I can swallow that for now. If I find you are lying to me, I'll tell you the same thing I told Sanders."

"What was that?"

"This. I'm in this case for the long haul. I intend to solve it, with or without help from law enforcement and if anyone I've come in contact with is on the dirty side of the deal,, including you, they are going to go to prison. Hiring people to get tough with me won't make me roll over. Money won't make me quit. I hope when this is over we can still drink a beer together and be friends."

"We will be." He said. "And if you want to go for lunch now, I'll drink a beer with you and I'll buy it."

He was smiling a big smile when he said it.

"OK" I said. "Give me my phone and let's go get a beer."

He opened a drawer in his desk and handed me a sealed manila envelope.

"It'll take some cleaning, and maybe a technician before you can use it," he said.

CHAPTER 31

It was almost three o'clock when I got back to my room. We had drank more than one beer and I didn't feel like pursuing anything else so I relaxed and had a good time with Donahue and some of the other Peoria detectives. I had the uncanny feeling that some of the homicide boys were alert and trying to pick up something that would tie me to Billy's murder.

Back at the motel, I changed into swimming trunks, took a quick dip in the pool, and spent an hour looking through the yellow pages for someone to clean my phone. I still had the one I'd bought after the ordeal with Billy, but it was a cheap one. I never thought I'd spend nearly a grand for a phone, but it had features that came in handy in my PI work.

I finally found a place and called it. The guy I talked to said he thought they could fix it and make it work again, but I'd have to take it back to the place I bought it to get them to set up my old number. I didn't know a thing about phones so I agreed. He said they closed at 4 so I got dressed and drove the two miles to the strip mall where the repair shop was located.

"What the heck did you do, drop it in a sewer?" The guy asked me, manila envelope extended as far from his face as his arm would allow, and holding his nose with his other hand.

"No, it got thrown in the river," I said.

"On purpose?"

"Yeah," I said. "The guy that threw it is dead now."

"I don't blame you," he told me, "I'd kill the son-of-a-bitch that threw my I phone in the river, too."

"Can you fix it?"

"If we can't, no one around here can," he said, opening the envelope.

"When can I get it back?"

"Three days," he said. "Today's Tuesday, how about Friday, noon?"

"I'll be back," I said. "How much is it going to cost me?"

"Probably a C-note," he said.

"OK," I said, and turned and walked towards the door.

"Hey, wait a minute," he yelled.

I turned back

"Yeah?"

"This isn't an Apple I phone."

"It isn't?"

"Nah...it's a Samsung. Resembles an I phone, but not nearly as good a phone, in my opinion."

"Are you sure?"

"Hey, man. I'd know a Galaxy from an I phone any time."

I stood there for a minute, thinking. It was possible, but not probable, that Donahue's divers had found someone else's phone near where Billy threw mine. I couldn't even begin to estimate the odds of that. *Then I came to the only possible solution. Billy had thrown his phone in the river and kept mine, either intentionally or by accident.*

"Can you fix it?"

"Sure. Not a lot of difference in the design. If we can't fix it......."

"Yeah, I know, no one can." I finished for him. "Same time frame?"

"Unless you want to expedite it. In that case it'll be $175."

"And when can I get it back?"

"Tomorrow morning, ten o'clock."

"Guaranteed?"

"If it's not ready by ten tomorrow, I'll knock of $50." He handed me his card. I glanced at it.

"World's Best Phone Repair." His number and name. Robert "Techno" Beasley.

"I'll be here at 10." I said.

I was more than a little bit anxious to get that phone back. Billy had thrown his own phone in the river instead of mine. That meant my Apple I phone was amongst Billy's possessions, and the phone I'd be picking up at 10 tomorrow might have a lot of information pertinent to a missing suitcase.

But for now, I wanted to see if I could find my own cell phone.

I drove to Billy's old pad and asked the landlady if she had seen a cell phone in Billy's room the morning she found his body.

She stammered and turned her head away from me, exhaled a dark cloud of cigarette smoke, coughed a phlegmatic, hoarse cough, and held up one finger as if to say, "wait a second."

I waited.

"Nope," she finally got out. I sensed she was lying.

I opened my wallet and flipped it to my PI badge.

"It's a ten year sentence at Joliet for removing evidence from a crime scene," I said

She coughed louder and longer.

I had no idea what the penalty in Illinois might be for removing evidence, but I played it a bit further.

"I'd hate to see a nice lady like you die in jail. They don't have any treatment for lung cancer there, they just let people die. Painful death, lung cancer. A friend of mine died of it"

She coughed louder.

"Of course if evidence has been taken from Billy's room, we'll find out about it. Particularly a cell phone. All we have to do is find out if any calls were made from that phone and trace them by the cell tower records."

I thought she was going to choke to death trying to confess.

"I...I... (cough, cough) I...(cough some more)."

"I forgot to get my camera from my car," I said. "I'll be back in a minute to take some pictures of Billy's room. We need pictures to help us find out who killed him."

I turned and walked out her front door and back to the rental car. I purposefully let her see me pull my phone out as I rattled off the number of the phone I suspected she might have found, loud enough that she would think I was keying that number.

I glanced over my shoulder as I walked down her sidewalk and I have never seen an old woman move so fast in my life. She disappeared from view for about ten seconds, then I saw a blur as she came back to the front hallway and disappeared up the stairs. I took my time, I didn't want her to have a heart attack running up and down the stairs.

I watched the reflection in the car windows and when I saw a blur of movement come down the stairs, through the hall landing, and back into her living room, I got my camera from the trunk of the car and walked slowly back up to her door and knocked again.

"Ma'am?"

She came to the door, gasping for air.

"Yes, sir?"

"Is it all right if I photograph Billy's room?"

"Sure, officer," she panted, opened the door and pointed up the stairway.

"Thank you." I said.

I walked up the stairs as slowly as my anxiety would let me. The door had been fixed, but it was unlocked, and I opened it and stepped inside Billy's room. It had been cleaned. Clean towels on the rack in the bathroom. Clean blanket on the cot.

And there in the middle of the cot was my cell phone.

CHAPTER 32

As I left, the old lady wheezed a partial explanation.

"That pretty lady that came earlier today might have left it there."

"What pretty lady? What did she look like?"

She described the woman and I thought immediately of someone I had talked to not too long ago.

"Had you ever seen her before?"

"Yes, she was here the night Billy was shot. She came to see him, but he wasn't home, so she left."

I didn't even bother stopping long enough to thank the landlady for letting me photograph Billy's room. The park where I had visited on my first trip to Peoria, when I looked up the motor vehicle department address, was nearby, and I drove to it, parked the car and hurried to the bench.

The first thing I did was to check recent calls. There were some numbers but no names, so Billy hadn't put anyone in my contacts list. I checked recent text messages and found one that was very interesting.

"I guess you know that my attempt to get rid of the guy from LA has failed. He found me and took me to Donahue. I spent a week in lock-up until Ford bailed me out."

And then from someone to Billy:

"Never mind that, Billy. Ford wants to know why you think you can still blackmail him?"

"He masterminded the heist. You know it, and I know it."

"Can you prove that?"

"I think I can."

"And you still want money from me? How much this time?"

"I need five grand."

"OK, Billy. I'll give you the five grand, but this is the last time you get any from me. Get it from Ford. I can't pay you anymore, and you can't prove my involvement any more than you can prove his."

"When do I get the 5 G?"

"I'll bring it over tonight."

"What time?"

"Around ten. Will you be there or out gambling somewhere?"

"I'll make it a point to be here. And I've got a lead on the suitcase, might never need another penny."

"You know where the suitcase is? Where?"

"Not for sure, but I'll be checking it out soon. That's why I need the 5G."

"OK. See you at 10."

That ended the conversation. I looked at the number from which the text was sent, and wondered who it was that Billy was shaking down, and why. I could do a reverse look up on the number from my phone, but I dialed the number instead.

The phone on the other end rang twice, then a sweet sounding voice answered.

"Hello?"

I pressed the 'end call' button.

The voice belonged to Lenore West.

So Billy was blackmailing both Ford and Lenore West. Was Cory aware that Lenore was involved in the heist? Or more probably, Cory himself was involved and the two of them were being blackmailed, along with Ford.

I wondered what Billy had that would prove his statement. Ford would have to be stupid to pay blackmail to someone who couldn't produce evidence. So Billy had at one time the goods to blackmail Ford, but somehow he had lost it. Yet he still had enough to put the pinch on Lenore West and perhaps Cory, before he fed him to the pigs.

What could he have that would be incriminating enough to blackmail anyone?

I decided that a good place to start would be to ask Lenore West.

Just as I started to leave the park and go visit the lovely Widow West, I got a call on my cheap cell phone from my home office. My secretary told me that I had received a fax from a person named Charles DuPont marked Private and Priority. She wondered what she should do with it. I told her to read it to me.

"Kip: In regards to our telephone conversation a few days ago, the party mentioned by me was Martha Downing, her maiden name. Her married name was Martha Ford. She was the wife of Marion Ford, former CEO of a pharmaceutical supplier in Peoria, IL. She disappeared mysteriously shortly after her indictment. If you need any further information regarding the investigation of the case or outcome, I have notified your friend Happs at the Homestead PD and my friend, the ex-FBI agent who you met while fishing. Good Luck and keep in touch."

Holy Batman, Joker. Ford had his wife go to Florida and set up the supply company named FlorPharma. So there had never been a sale of the goods stolen in the Peoria heist, just a transfer. So there was no millions of dollars floating around somewhere waiting to be divided amongst the participants of the heist. And somehow, Billy Brooks, the lowest guy on the totem pole who participated in the big heist, had stumbled on the fact that no one was going to get a bundle of money. That is the thing that Billy was holding over Ford's head, whatever proof he had. The thought occurred to me that maybe Cory West and his lovely wife, and Rod Sanders, were left out of the loop and thus never received the payoff they expected. But Billy had something on them too, something that would put them away for their involvement in the heist. Something powerful enough to make someone want him dead. And whatever it was that Billy had was in a suitcase, hiding somewhere. Billy knew where the suitcase was, he just didn't have the means to get to it, so he was hitting Lenore West up for a final $5G to finance getting the suitcase.

I had an idea that I now held the key to the missing suitcase. Not the little key that would open it, but the clue that told me where the suitcase was hidden.

In an old Fruehauf trailer on an impound lot.

Now I needed to be very, very careful. At least two people, Sanders and Donahue, knew I was close to finding that suitcase and I am smart enough to know that as soon as I find it, my contract with Sanders won't be worth the paper it is written on. I'll be feeding the pigs out in the country. No one will ever find my body and no one will ever know anything about the missing Cory, except Donahue and my pal, Toby Smith. Donahue won't tell anyone, and Toby can't tell anyone without getting in a heap of trouble with the California Highway Patrol on an obstructing justice charge.

It was up to me to get that suitcase and get it back to LA and put it in the right hands. I wasn't sure I could trust anyone in the Peoria Police Department. Donahue may or may not be crooked, so I had my task in front of me. Deliver the suitcase to Toby Smith, but turn the Billy Brooks and the Cory West murders over to local authorities.

If Donahue wasn't dirty, I'd know it soon enough, and if he was, well, that would have to play out the best way.

Not only did I think I knew where the suitcase was hiding, but now I had a pretty good idea who killed Billy Brooks, and it wasn't Ford or Donahue.

CHAPTER 33

It was nearing nine o'clock when I parked the rental in the suburban neighborhood and got out. Crickets were chirping, insects of all kinds were singing in harmony. The late summer breeze from the south had temperatures hovering around seventy.

I had taken time to go over everything that I knew about this case very carefully in my old toboggan, turning dials, clicking little levers here and there, fine tuning it as much as my senses would let me. Nothing jumped out at me as being a final resolution, but a lot of things were making sense.

I didn't know what line of questioning I was going to take with the very attractive widow of Cory West, but I was pretty sure of one thing. She was involved in the whole apple cart up to her pretty little nose.

The West residence was a brick home in an upscale neighborhood. I didn't have any idea what it might be worth in Illinois dollars, but a similar house in a similar neighborhood in sunny California would be in the neighborhood of a couple of million dollars.

A light was on above the entry way and another in what was probably the living room. I rang the doorbell and waited.

When she saw me, she smiled. It was quite a change from the last time we had spoken. She had told me to take my foot out of her door.

"Mr. Yardley," she said. "Come in."

Said the spider to the fly.

"Good evening, ma'am." I said, in my politest voice.

"It's Lenore," she said.

"Ma'am?"

"Lenore," she said. "Quote the Raven, nevermore."

"Oh," I said. "Yes, ma'am. M-m-m Lenore. May I come in?"

Come into my parlor, said the spider to the fly.

"Yes, please," she said, holding the door open.

I went in. It was nicer to be able to talk to her from the inside, even though I still didn't know what I was going to say. Ad lib it, Yardley, I told myself.

"What brings you to see me at this hour, Mr. Yardley."

"Please, call me Kip."

"OK, Kip," she said. "Same question. What brings you to see me at this hour? Would you like to sit down?"

"Thank you."

I sat down in an armchair that looked like it might have been once used by Thomas Jefferson. It was comfortable.

"I was just wondering, Mrs. West, if you have heard from your husband?"

"No, as a matter of fact, I have not." She said.

"Have the police questioned you or have you talked to Detective Donahue?"

"No. Do you have any information about his whereabouts, Kip?"

"Do you think that Billy might know anything?"

Her head snapped up immediately.

"Billy's dead," she said.

"Oh yes, I'm sorry, I meant do you think Billy might have known?"

"How would he? Why would Billy Brooks know anything at all about Cory?"

"Well," I said, and decided to be blunt. "I'm pretty sure that Billy Brooks was killed by someone who might have some bearing on your husband's disappearance."

A look of relief spread across her face. I had purposefully told a little lie.

"Be honest," she said, "Do you think Cory is dead?"

Her eyes were looking directly into mine. It might be a long shot, but I was pretty sure that she knew Cory was dead.

"The last time I was here, you mentioned that you did the finances for you and Cory, and that you would know if he was in financial trouble."

"That's right."

"Well, it seems as if there is a pattern of withdrawals from your checking account, each amounting to about $5000, and occurring about every six months." I was really winging it now, but I wanted to try to get a reaction.

"How would you know about that?" She asked, rather too quickly. "I know that you are a private detective from Los Angeles, how would you have access to my bank account?"

That told me something. She knew who I was, and if she knew that, there was a huge chance that she knew why I was in Peoria, particularly since I had questioned her about the suitcase on my last visit.

"Let me ask a different question, did you go to Billy's room the night he was killed?"

That one really shook her. Her demeanor had been almost friendly then it changed to business only, now the look on her face told me it was going to be Katy bar the door.

"No." She said, coldly. "I wouldn't have any reason to see Billy on that night or any other night." She stood up and walked towards the door.

"I think you did," I said. There, it was out. Now I had to go through with it, or I would never be able to speak to Lenore West again. "I think that Billy knew something about you or Cory that you didn't want known. I think he was blackmailing you. The money that you withdrew from your checking account regularly was going to Billy, wasn't it?"

"I think you've spent enough time here, Mr. Yardley, please leave."

"I'll leave," I said. "But before I do, I wonder if you would mind reading a text conversation you had with Billy on my cell phone?"

He face went very pale.

"Or maybe you would rather I read it for you?"

I took out my phone and opened it to the text messages between her and Billy.

I read the first line, ("I guess you know that my attempt to get rid of the guy from LA has failed. He found me and took me to Donahue. I spent a week in lock-up until Ford bailed me out.")

A look of shock spread over her face.

"Would you like for me to read some more?"

I read the last few lines.

"When do I get the 5 G?"

"I'll bring it over tonight."

"What time?"

"Around ten."

"Here's what I think happened that night," I started, "You went to Billy's to pay him the 5G that he demanded. You got there early and Billy wasn't home yet. The landlady let you in, Billy wasn't there so you waited for Billy in his room. While you waited, you looked around the room and there in plain view, you found what you thought was Billy's cell phone, the one I'm holding in my hand."

She started to tremble.

"You didn't realize until that point that Cory would not be coming back, but you suspected it. You saw the scene that I recorded from the attic of the farm house. You saw Billy and Cory fight over Cory's gun, and you saw what happened."

She stopped near the door and turned away from me and brought both hands up to her face. Her shoulders were shaking.

"You dropped the phone on the cot when Billy came in, picked up my gun, the one Billy had taken from me, and shot Billy. You wiped your prints off of the gun and left, but forgot the phone. The cops found my gun and arrested me."

"You are the pretty lady the landlady mentioned to me, you went back the next day to see if you could get the phone. She thought it might have been your phone, you thought it was Billy's phone, but you see, strange coincidences happen. It is my phone. And it was my gun that killed Billy."

"Do you mean this gun?"

She turned and I saw my gun in her hand. It was pointed right at my chest.

"Maybe Billy couldn't get rid of the man from LA, but I can. You came here and questioned me about a suitcase and when I told you that I didn't know anything about a suitcase, you got rough with me. You pushed me around. I got my gun from my concealed carry spot and shot you. How does that sound, Mr. LA Private Eye? Sanders said you were very smart. In a pig's eye!"

"I don't think you can get away with it, Lenore," I said, trying to buy some time and think of something.

"Oh I'll get away with it all right," she said. She held the gun steady on my chest with her right hand, and with her left she ripped her blouse from the top button to the bottom. Buttons flew everywhere. She grabbed the left side of her brassier and yanked down hard. It came off and her pretty breast bounced high then jiggled to a stop.

"Nice," I said. "But aren't you forgetting something?"

"What did I forget, Smartass?"

"I've recorded everything you just said, and pushed the send button. Your scenario for shooting me has all been transmitted to my LA office. And how will you explain that you shot me with my own gun?" I was lying through my teeth, but it might work.

Her face paled further.

"I don't believe you, Yardley. You're smart, but not that smart."

There is an old self defense trick. When faced with no other choice but to try to get your opponent's eyes to glance away, even for a split second, if you have something in your hands, toss it.

"Would you like to see?" I said and tossed the phone in her direction.

It worked. When she glanced at the cell phone, I leapt towards her right side, crouching low. The gun went off, the noise echoed in the entry way.

I heard the mirror in the entryway explode with the sound of falling glass as I grabbed her right wrist in my right hand. The sound of her arm breaking across my knee wasn't quite as loud as the gun, but her scream was.

CHAPTER 34

With one hand I picked up the phone, absently praying that it hadn't broken when it hit the floor, all the while holding both of Lenore West's wrist with the other hand. I maneuvered behind the chair in which I had sat moments before and jerked her down in it, she was still screeching in pain. I punched Donahue's number and waited, hoping desperately that he would be in his office at this late hour.

The phone rang as I sent up a little prayer that he would be there.

No one answered but after four rings the dispatcher picked up.

I told her I needed to speak to Detective Donahue and that it was urgent.

Another phone rang, probably his home.

"Donahue."

My prayer was answered.

"Can you get an ambulance and a squad car over here to Lenore West's house ASAP?"

"Kip? What the hell is going on?"

"She just tried to kill me, is all," I said. "I've got pretty good proof that she killed Billy Brooks. She's got a broken right arm, self defense on my part. She got it when I took my gun away from her."

"Your gun? How did she get your gun?"

"She didn't, Billy did, remember?"

"But she got the drop on you?"

"Damn it, Donahue, are you going to send an ambulance or let this woman suffer? Get a squad car over here and I'll answer all of your questions next time I see you."

"Wait there, Yardley,

"Not a chance," I said. "I've got more work to do, and I don't have time to sit in your office all night. I'll clue you in next time I see you."

"I can put out a APB and you'll be charged," he said.

"Go ahead, Donahue. Then you can wrap this case up all by yourself. I'm sure you've figure it all out after all these years."

He was silent.

"OK, you win."

I hit the "call end" button and stuck the phone in my pocket.

The reading lamp on the table had a long extension cord to the wall. I jerked the plug out of the wall and dropped the lamp to the floor, put my foot on it and pulled up hard on the cord. It came lose after two attempts. I tied Lenore's hands behind her with half of the cord and ran the end through the arm of the chair and tied it. She wouldn't be going anywhere without dragging Thomas Jefferson's chair with her.

I picked up my gun and stuck it under my belt in the small of my back, turned on every light in the house, and walked out into cool Peoria evening.

CHAPTER 35

I needed a drink and a rest. I sat at the bar in the lounge of the motel and had two martinis. I could feel the tension escape my body. It was almost over. I had Billy's killer and that would free me from the Grand Jury. I was pretty sure I knew where the mysterious suitcase resided.

It was 8:30 Peoria time. I thought about calling Sanders and confronting him with my suspicions just to rattle his cage to see what fell out. Instead, I called the phone technician.

"Techno Beasley," he answered.

"This is Kip Yardley, the guy whose phone got tossed in the river."

"Oh yeah. I'm working on it now. Almost done. It'll be ready by 10 for sure."

"Can I get it tonight? I have an appointment tomorrow I forgot about."

"Well, I might be able to finish it in an hour. No guarantee though."

"You mean no guarantee you can finish or no guarantee on the job?"

"No guarantee I can finish. All of my work is guaranteed for 3 months."

"Good enough," I said. "I'm on my way over. If you finish in an hour there'll be a bonus."

"If I finish in an hour there'll be another expedite fee," he said.

"Fine." I said, and ended the call. Greed. The ruination of the nation.

I didn't think two martinis would seriously impair my driving, but never-the-less I was a little more cautious when I pulled out of the parking lot, looking both ways and checking all around me, including my rear view mirror. Just as I pulled out I noticed a cars lights come on in the lot and it pulled out behind me. I was being tagged.

Probably Donahue's pals keeping an eye on me at his request, I thought.

At least that's what I thought until the car passed me on my left and I caught the glimpse of a gun barrel. I hit the brake hard and the car zipped ahead of me just as the blast from the gun sprayed shot in front of me. I reached for my 9 that I had stuck in my belt. I stomped on the gas and cut the wheel to the left nearing the left rear side of the car.

The driver saw that I was trying to pull even so he quickly maneuvered the car to the left and blocked me. It was a two way street and there was a car approaching toward me so I cut right and waited. I didn't think I could catch the car, it was gaining ahead of me, so I eased off of the gas and pulled into a side street and called Donahue.

"Someone just shot at me from a Nissan Altima, black or dark blue. I was headed north on 5th street, near the motel."

He whistled.

"You'd be better off coming in to see me, Kip. Someone wants you out of the picture."

"I'll bet you got your badge from a Cracker Jack box, Donahue." I said.

"You're a better second baseman than you are detective," he replied, but I could hear a little humor in his voice. "You coming in?"

"No. I've got an errand to run. When that's over, I'll sleep on it, then another errand tomorrow, then I'll come wrap this thing up for you."

"Be careful," he said.

I pulled back out and headed north on 5th again, towards the phone repair shop. I didn't worry about the execution attempt. Whoever pulled it wasn't likely to come back and try again, knowing I was aware and expecting trouble.

Minutes later I parked in front of the shop and got out, noticing that the lights were still on in the shop. As I entered, Techno Beasley looked up from his work bench and stood up, walked towards the counter carrying a phone.

"Done?"

"No, not yet," he said, then motioned with the phone. "This one's mine. I'm just calling my wife to tell her I'll be late."

"Yeah, honey," he said into the phone. "I'll be home by eleven for sure. Don't wait up for me, I'll stop and get a sandwich somewhere. OK. Love you too."

"Give me another half an hour," he told me.

I had no idea what the hell he needed to do but if it made the phone usable it might be worth it.

"Are text messages and recordings still on it?"

"That's what I'm on now," he said. "I'm hoping I can retrieve them."

"So am I," I said.

"Have a seat, do you want coffee?"

"No thanks." I sat down in the waiting area. He returned to his bench.

I was dozing off when I heard Billy's voice.

"Yes, Sir, Mr. Ford," he said, plain as day.

I woke up startled.

"Got it," Techno said.

"Recording?"

"Yeah. You wanna hear it?"

"Can I listen to it later?"

"Sure. It's there, you just have to play it."

"What about texts?" I asked.

"Yep." He said. "Got them too."

"You're a genius," I told him. "What's my damages?"

"Two hundred," he said.

I gave him my credit card for the two hundred and added a twenty in cash.

"Thanks a million," I said.

"Wish it was," he said. "You're welcome. Thanks for the tip."

I put the phone in my pocket and left.

As much as I wanted to hear what Billy Brooks was telling Marion Ford, I waited until I arrived back at the motel and was safely ensconced in my room before playing it.

"Yes, Sir, Mr. Ford," Billy said.

"If you can get that on your phone, a picture is worth a thousand words, Billy,"

Ford said.

"I'll get it," Billy said.

"Call me at home when you have it, OK?"

"I don't have your home number," Billy said.

Ford rattled it off.

"Wait, I can't remember it, I'll have to write it down," Billy told him.

Ford gave Billy his home phone number again, and Billy wrote it down, repeated it to make sure he had it right.

"I'll call you," Billy said.

"Good work, Billy," Ford said. "I'll see that you get a bonus for this."

The phone was silent.

I hit stop on the phone and then menu and looked for pictures. I found pictures under gallery and then 'videos' under that. There was only one. I pushed 'play' and watched Sanders and Cory putting containers of pills in a suitcase. There was not much background noise and I could hear it very plain.

"Where will we sell them?" Cory asked.

"That won't be hard," Sanders said. "We just need to get them back home. I'll get in touch with some boys in Chicago. There's a lot of money here, Cory. Let's hope Ford never realizes what we're doing."

Something didn't seem right. I was watching the video, it was Sanders and Cory, loading plastic containers of pills in a suitcase. They were taking them from a large cardboard box and placing them neatly in the suitcase.

It took me almost a half of a minute to realize what I was seeing.

Sanders wasn't in a wheel chair.

The phone was silent as the video played on. Then I watched as Sanders put the last container in place and zipped up the suitcase.

The heist took place long after Sanders left college. And he was injured in a football game while in college. That's what caused his paralysis. But here he was standing tall, helping himself to some pills from the Peoria heist. I couldn't get the connection.

Why was he now in a wheel chair in Simi Valley, California?

When I ran my computer background check on Sanders before taking the case, did it miss something? I needed to do some more checking, not that it really mattered, but because I have a real acute sense of curiosity.

I turned off the phone and went to bed. Tomorrow is another day.

CHAPTER 36

After breakfast in the motel I drove directly to the trailer storage lot. There was a small crowd of people there. An auctioneer had a loud speaker system going and I could hear his steady chant. I listened for a few seconds and was able to determine that it wasn't the trailers that were being auctioned. Since the trailers were my main concern, I took my time parking the car and sauntered to a table where a clerk sat taking names of people who intended to bid.

I signed in, went through the regular process of showing financial backing to bid, and waited near the trailer where I had found Marion Ford's phone number.

It was nearly an hour later, all kinds of good stuff had passed under the auctioneers gavel. Tools, a few automobiles, a pick- up truck, and a lot of electronics. I bid on a portable electric drill, some sheet metal shears, a hammer and screwdriver, all part of a lot, in a metal tool box. I got the lot for peanuts and carried it with me. I had no idea what I was going to bid for the trailer, but hoped that no-one would be interested in an old Fruehauf trailer with dry rot tires. When they finally got around to announcing the sale of the trailer I was interested in, I felt more confident. The first one had gone for $2000 and I could see no reason why the second would sell for more.

I was wrong. I learned something I had missed on my two trips to the storage yard. The first trailer was a common cargo trailer. The second one was a refrigerated unit. It was worth more. The bidding started at a grand and soon hit two grand. I was bidding along with three or four others. The auctioneers prattle was fluid and I heard when the bids changed. When the "going, going, going for $2885" reached my ear, I raised my hand and shouted, "twenty nine hundred."

Immediately someone said $2925 and someone else said $2950.

I had determined that I could go as high as $4500 but not a penny higher. I wished that Donahue was with me so he could invoke his police power and end the bid. But he wasn't.

I decided to gamble.

"Three thousand."

Silence.

A little more prattle, "I've got three grand in my hand, who'll bid more, who'll go four?"

Still silence.

"I've got three, who'll go three twenty five? Three and a quarter looking for a quarter. Who'll give me three thousand twenty five?"

No one said a word. I thought I saw a hand go up a few yards away but the man was just scratching his head or straightening his baseball cap. He didn't speak.

"Going once for three grand, going once. Going twice at three grand, going twice."

I held my breath.

"Sold for three thousand dollars to the man in the shorts and tee shirt."

I got a few stares out of that, but now I was the proud owner of a fifty foot refrigerated trailer with dry rot tires and had until five o:clock to get it out of the impound lot.

I went back to the table and signed on the dotted line. If I failed to get the trailer moved by 5, I would forfeit twenty five percent of my bid, seven hundred and fifty bucks.

I signed on the line again, agreeing to the forfeiture clause. I had been watching the guys who were bidding against me and picked out the one who looked like he knew the most about trailers. He had a white baseball cap with the words "Lightning Trucking" in blue letters, and "We move fast" in red letters.

"Hope there's no hard feelings," I said to him as he passed me.

"Hell no, man. I ain't got enough refrigerated freight to fill that damned thing anyway. If I don't get another contract soon, I'll be selling the ones I got."

"Thanks."

"No problem. Who you drive for? You don't look like a trucker, no offense, but most of my drivers don't wear shorts and tee shirts advertising a golf course."

"Oh I'm not a trucker," I said. "I really need some advice though. I have to move this thing by five. Can you recommend someone to haul it out for me?"

"Where are you moving it to?"

I hadn't thought of that. Some things I am good at and some I am not good at. I can usually handle myself pretty good against a man twice my size in physical combat, but when it comes to planning small details like where am I going to store a 50 foot trailer, I come up short.

"Not more than 100 miles," I said, winging it.

"Here's my card," he said, handing me a card with the same information that was on his cap, but a name and a phone number as well. "I'll move it for $5 a mile up to 100, you provide insurance. After a hundred I'll have to drop it, I won't be able to take it further."

"Deal," I said, extending my hand. "I'm Kip Yardley, from Los Angeles."

He shook my hand with a grip like the Incredible Hulk.

"You want 'er moved, huh?"

"Yes. Will you be able to move it before five?"

"Hell, Kip Yardley, I'll move it now. I've got a tractor out in the parking lot. If the hoses aren't dry rotted, we'll hook up and haul 'er out right now."

"Great," I said.

"Cash deal?"

"Oh yeah," I said and opened my wallet. I try to carry a grand in a hidden place in my wallet, for emergency purposes. I pulled out five one hundred dollar bills and extended them towards him.

"Not now," he said. "When we drop it, I'll collect."

"OK."

"I'll get the tractor," he said. I watched as he crossed the street to a parking lot and climbed up in a big Kenworth, cranked it and sat there a minute while the clattering of the diesel engine reached my ears.

Suddenly I felt panic surge through me. Where could I have this damned thing towed to?

My mind raced around like cars at a NASCAR meet. I don't know what made me glance at my hands but I was standing there with my wallet in one hand and $500 in the other. I put the money away and as I did I noticed a card. I pulled it out and looked at it. It was a plain business card, not much on it.

"C. Stevenson, Farmer" with his phone number was all it said, but if pictures are worth a thousand words, these words were worth fifty thousand pictures of Lincoln.

I punched in the number and he answered.

"Howdy, Stevenson here."

"Hello Mr. Stevenson," I said. "I hope you'll remember me, I'm Kip Yardley, an investigator from L.A. I talked to you about your house you had rented to Billy Brooks."

"Well howdy," he said. "Yeah, I recollect talking to you out on the porch. What can I do for you?"

"Well, Sir, I just bought a fifty foot trailer, and I need a place to store it for a few days. I was wondering if you've got a spot on your farm where you wouldn't mind if I parked it?"

"Fifty footer, huh? Well, I reckon it wouldn't hurt anything to park it out by the barn on that property you asked me about."

"The barn on the place you had rented to Billy Brooks?"

"Yep. If that ain't satisfactory, I'll move some equipment, a combine and an old tractor, and you can park it here at my house."

"That would do just fine, Mr. Stevenson," I said, "The barn at the Brooks rental place. I'll pay you to store it there until it's moved."

"No you won't either," he said. "Just stop and have lunch with an old man. I get lonesome here sometimes."

"I'll do that, Mr. Stevenson, and thank you."

"No problem. Glad I could help."

No problem, the man said. I looked up and the diesel tractor was coming across the street. The man just saved me $750 and he said it was no problem. My faith in humanity went back up 100 points.

The big rig stopped and Lighting looked down at me from the cab.

"Find out where you want it?" he asked.

"Yes, I did," I yelled up at him over the rattle of the engine. "If you'll just follow me I'll lead you to the place."

"You lead, I'll follow," Lightning said. "Give me ten minutes to hook up and inspect the tow."

He revved the engine and rattled on up to the trailer. I waited.

CHAPTER 37

It didn't take me long to get a 4 x 8 ft piece of sheet metal removed from the inside of the trailer near the spot where I had previously removed a small piece with Ford's phone number written on it in pencil.

What I found behind the sheet metal is what I had been looking for since the first day I arrived in Peoria. A suitcase.

In it I found plastic containers. In the containers I found pills.

I counted the containers. There was 150 of them. I guessed there were about 200 pills in each container. Thirty thousand pain killers. Street value of about $65 each. Nearly two million dollars worth of drugs if sold on the street.

In a plastic bag next to the suitcase I found nearly ten thousand dollars in $100 bills. There was a rip in the bag and hanging on a rivet near the top of the opening was a piece of plastic. Someone who had hastily shoved the bag in the air space next to the suitcase had caught it on a rivet and the bag had torn. Part of a hundred dollar bill had been torn and stuck to the small sliver I had cut out and sent to my friend Richard Rheames. I owed Richard a World Series game for that find.

I put the pills back in the leather suitcase and zipped it shut. I put the tools back in the box I had carried them in and scooted suitcase and box to the rear of the trailer then I got the bag of $100 bills and walked back towards sunlight at the trailer door.

Someone was waiting for me there.

That someone had an automatic pistol pointed at my midsection.

"That's far enough, Yardley."

The voice was high and effeminate. I recognized it immediately. Marion Ford.

"How did you find me?" I asked.

"It wasn't hard. I have someone who works for me keep a tail on you."

"Let me guess," I said. "That someone also took a shot at me with a shotgun. If he had killed me then, you wouldn't be here now. Right?"

"Close, Yardley." He said.

"I'll guess again. It was Stronheim, right?"

"We had you pegged right, Yardley. You are smart."

"Not smart enough," I said, "If I had been smart I would have been watching for a tail, since I knew my part in this whole caper was to lead someone to the suitcase."

Ford remained silent.

"How does Stronheim play in this? I know he served some time with Billy Brooks, but what was his part in the grand scheme of things?"

"He owned a trailer repair shop in Georgia." Ford said. "Billy stole the suitcase full of pills from Sanders and West. I gave him instructions to the repair shop in Georgia and told him to put it where you just found it. I was going to bring the trailer back to our warehouse, so that was the safest way to transport the pills. Billy sold ten grand worth of pills to Stronheim and put all but $500 in a plastic bag and stuck it in with the suitcase. I'm guessing he planned on recovering the bag when he brought me the suitcase. Stronheim got busted for selling some of the pills and the police came to me. I went to visit him in prison, made an agreement, and when he got out he came to me for a job."

"But Billy got stopped by Georgia police, the trailer was thought to be stolen, and they impounded it?"

"He wouldn't tell them it belonged to my company, they contacted Peoria police and turned the trailer over to them. No one but Billy and I knew the pills were in the trailer."

"How did you lose something as big as a trailer?" I asked.

"Peoria turned the trailer over to the FBI. They put it in the impound lot and after five years, Peoria PD was given title. That's where we lost it."

"So how did West and Sanders get wind of it?"

"They didn't know it was in the trailer. Billy was contacted by Sanders shortly after he got out of prison but he wanted Sanders to cut him in on it. He made up the story about putting it behind the drywall in the house he lived in to keep Sanders interested. He figured Sanders could help him find the trailer."

"And Stronheim knew about the suitcase but not about the trailer?"

"You've got it. Billy had him remove a section of trailer skin to look for bad wiring. While the section was off, Billy hid the pills and the cash inside."

"Why did you send him to blast me? You would have never found the suitcase without me."

"I've had my eye out for the trailer for years. I'm the one who sent Billy the notice of sale. He was supposed to buy the trailer, not you. You weren't of any more use to me until today. But I didn't send him to kill you. He must have thought that by this time I had the suitcase or knew where it was."

I had to keep him talking until I figured out a way to disarm him.

"So Sanders convinced West to have his agency hire a Private Detective to assist in finding the suitcase, thinking that a good PI would lead them to it. West went to his friend on the Peoria Police Department, Donahue. They came up with me. Sanders hired me to watch his pool party, then offered me the job of finding the suitcase, after getting dunked in his own pool."

"The scene at the pool was fixed." Ford said.

"Fixed?"

"Yes. The man and woman who were arguing were actors. The woman was Sanders ex-wife and the man was her boyfriend. Sanders just figured you'd break up the argument and throw the actors out and that would give him the opportunity to offer you the job he really wanted you to do, find the suitcase. He didn't fake the dunking in the pool, but that worked out better for him."

"Let me ask you this, Mr. Ford," I said, stalling. I wasn't sure what Ford was going to do with me, but I figured he'd kill me then lock my body in the trailer.

"What are your intentions now? Do you kill me, take the suitcase and run? How are you going to get rid of my body? Lock me in the trailer and let me rot?"

"That might not be the best of ideas, Yardley. Someone might have knowledge that I trailed you here, and finding your body would be dangerous to me. Stronheim will be here in a few minutes, then we intend to feed the pigs."

"You know about that?"

"Yes. Billy told me."

I was thinking that I had better find a way to overpower Ford before Stronheim returned. One man is easier to take down than two.

He was standing three feet away from the end of the trailer and I was still up in it. The plastic bag full of hundreds, the suitcase full of pills, and the box full of tools were at my feet.

I kicked the bag of money.

It flew straight at Ford's face, just like I had hoped.

Ford threw both hands up to protect his face and I dove at his chest.

My head hit his chest right below his neck and the air whooshed out of him. We both hit the ground hard, me with my arms around his neck. He landed on his back, his right hand, holding the gun, went flying up and behind his head, hitting the ground hard. By that time my right hand was headed at his chin.

The gun went off just as my fist slammed into Ford's chin, and the sound of fist hitting chin was muffled by the gunshot. Ford went out like one of Rocky's opponents.

I dragged Ford to the rental car and left him in the back seat, hands cuffed behind him with the chain looped through the headrest brackets.

As I backed out of the car I heard the sound of a car door opening behind me.

I turned in time to see Stronheim get out of the car holding a shotgun. He leveled it at me and I thought I was dead.

"I see you found it," he said.

"I see you found me."

He approached my car, holding the shotgun level with my head.

"What did you do to Ford?"

"Knocked him out. He'll come to in a minute. What are you going to do with me?"

"Didn't Ford tell you? We're going to feed the pigs. Then we'll take the suitcase and cash, I'll drive your car to the airport and come back with a tractor and haul this trailer down to the river. There's a place where I can back it in, release it, and no one will ever find it unless the river goes dry."

"Yeah, I'm familiar with that place. Billy damned near killed me there."

"We might lock you in the trailer, kill two birds with one stone, so to speak."

I heard a groan and glanced at Ford. He shook his head and yelled at Stronheim.

"Get me out of these handcuffs," he screamed.

"Give me the key, Yardley."

"No deal, Stronheim. You want it, you'll have to kill me here."

"Shoot that son of a bitch." Ford said.

I was twenty feet from Stronheim and there was absolutely nothing I could do to avoid getting killed. Sweat popped out on my forehead immediately.

Stronheim raised the shotgun and pointed it at my head.

I heard a boom.

A streak of red exploded from Stronheim's chest. He pitched forward, the shotgun still in his dead hands.

I glanced towards the sound. A puff of smoke caught my eye. It came from a high powered rifle held in the gnarled old hands of Clifford Stevenson, Peoria's greatest pig farmer. A man I owed my life to. He hollered down at me from the barn loft window.

"You OK Yardley?"

* * *

I sat in Donahue's office, going over the entire scenario. I told him the whole story, starting with the pool party and ending with Stevenson saving my hide.

"You're a lucky man, Kip. Stevenson was having some trouble with coyotes killing his hogs. He just happened to be in that barn loft, otherwise you'd be pig poop by now"

"God works in mysterious ways," I said. "And so do Private Eyes."

Then I thought of something I had pondered over.

"Why would Sanders come to you to get my name? Did you know that he was involved in the heist?"

"I knew he worked for the company," Donahue said. "I figured it wouldn't hurt anything. I didn't know for sure what his involvement was, but I had some feelers put out on him. He told me that he was working for Cory's firm to find out who did the heist. I had worked some with Cory but I didn't know he was in on the heist, I thought his job with the insurance company was his only interest."

"Why did he pretend to be paralyzed?" I asked.

"He had a thing going. He was playing the pain game with about thirty different doctors, both here and in California, claiming he was paralyzed in a football accident in college. The doctors would write him prescriptions for pain killers, mostly ocycontone, and he would sell the pills. His income was boosted by about $50,000 a year by selling pain pills. The wheel chair was all part of his act. I guess he learned how to act from his ex-wife. She even wheeled him around to the different doctor's in California to get his prescriptions. He probably cut her in on the profits. Our friend Toby Smith has picked Sanders up and is holding him for extradition to Illinois."

"How long have you known about Sanders?"

"We've been keeping an eye on a lot of people, Kip. The one guy we thought was innocent turned out to be the biggest crook. Ford funneled the stolen drugs to his wife in Florida. She sold them to doctor's there. They had a good thing going until the cops got wise down there. She was indicted, but disappeared shortly afterward. I suspect she met an untimely demise at the hands of Ford."

"Do you have a picture of her?"

"Yeah, there's one here in the file somewhere." He spun around and opened a drawer of a filing cabinet and ruffled through the folders.

Facing me again, he scooted a picture across the desk.

It sure looked a lot like Ford's maid.

"One more question," I said.

"Go ahead, Colombo."

"How did Ford know I was coming to Indianapolis to see him?"

"Probably from Stronheim," Donahue said. "I'm guessing, but if Stronheim was tailing you and saw you headed towards Indianapolis, he probably followed you and tipped off Ford."

"Then he took a potshot at me in Indianapolis," I said.

"You never told me someone tried to shoot you while you were there."

"You didn't ask." I said. "To tell you the truth, I thought you might have tipped him off."

"Hell, he called me and told me you were there. He said he heard on the news that we wanted you for Billy's death."

"Well, I'm just glad it's over," I said. "Now I can get back to California, relax a week or so, play some golf."

"I was hoping you'd play ball with us Saturday," he said. "We're playing a team from Louisville for the police championship."

"No thanks, Donahue. I'm a detective but not a cop. And I'll never get the fifty g's that Sanders agreed to pay me for the suitcase, so I've got to work for a living. Will you reimburse me the 3 grand for the trailer?"

He stood up.

"We'll have to hold it for evidence. I guess we can reverse that auction sale. You'll get your 3 grand back."

"Thanks," I said.

"Hey, thanks for helping me with this case, Kip. I've got two more cases you can help me with."

"What kind of cases? I might be interested."

He slapped me on the back.

"Both of them are Bud Lite."

THE END

This is the 8th book by Don Yarber. Bodies and Beaches, Corpses and Canyons, Death and Deep Waters, Evil and Everglades, and now In a Pig's Eye are all PI mysteries featuring Kip Yardley.

The Sign Killer, Train to the Sun, and Joint Effort in Death are stand alone mysteries. Don lives near Morganfield, KY with his wife, Shirley, and their dog, Dottie.

www.ingramcontent.com/pod-product-compliance
Lightning Source LLC
Chambersburg PA
CBHW060540180626
46817CB00002B/664